This book is a work of fiction and any resemblances to persons, living or dead, places, events, or locales is purely coincidental. They are productions of the author's imagination and used fictitiously.

To obtain permissions, write *support@zanybooks.com*

To purchase more fine e-books like the one you're reading, go to *http://zanybooks.com*.

Table of Contents

Meeting People

One Night Stands

Unusual Bedfellows

Breaking Up

"Apartment in the Valley" first appeared in Riverbabble #6
"Dansing" and "Bloody Marys" first appeared in Unlikely Stories
"Shave and a Haircut" first appeared in Echos, Summer, 1994
"Wrong Kind of Music" first appeared in Moxie, 2000

Part I: Meeting People

Apartment in the Valley

(Adapted from the novel *In Search of Aimai Cristen)*

They say one can find something to do twenty-four hours a day in Los Angeles. Maybe. And maybe one can't find anything to do at all.

The apartment manager told me I could expect to find girls sitting around the pool in the evenings, and so when evening came and the lights went on in the courtyard I sat listening for sounds from below. All was silent apart from the complex's Muzak, on continuously, which played "Barefoot in the Park," and something that might once have been "Lucy in the Sky with Diamonds."

I peeked out the window finally, turning my back on my rented bed, my stereo, and the endless rolling contours of the sprayed acoustic ceiling, only to see a deserted courtyard and the safety lights reflected from the surface of the still, green pool.

"I'm not going to stay here and be alone." Was I talking to myself or to an imaginary cat? Shutting the apartment door firmly behind me, I stepped out on the landing that ran along the three long sides of the deserted courtyard. I knocked first on the door to my right. "Yes," came a girl's voice.

"I'm your next-door neighbor."

"I'm busy right now; could you come back later?"

"Sure. I'll be back," I added to the closed door.

I repeated the same procedure at the door to the left of my apartment. No one responded. From below, I heard a man's voice call, "They're not in." I looked down to see Arnie, the manager of the apartment complex, looking up at me. "What are you doing?" Arnie demanded.

I explained I was just checking with my neighbor.

"Well, they're not in." He stood there, hands in his pockets, and waited for me to go back inside my apartment.

"It's a quiet evening," I said conversationally.

Arnie was unresponsive. "People are trying to eat their supper," he replied as if to suggest he would be inside eating his supper if he did not have to be on duty policing me.

"Thank you," I said, feeling that perhaps a thank-you was expected.

Arnie glared, his face bright red in the reflections from the pool light. "Well. Aren't you going in?"

I scurried inside my apartment and waited just inside the entranceway until I heard Arnie's door close below. Then, I walked outside again and tiptoed down the length of the long motel landing. When I felt I was out of Arnie's earshot, I knocked on an apartment door.

"Yes?" A man came to the door, bare-chested, carrying a can of beer. He stood blocking the doorway, the sweat shining on his muscular body. A slim blond was setting plates on the table inside. She did not look up. "Yeah?" the man said again.

"I just moved in. I was trying to meet people in the building."

"What's he want honey?"

"Nothing." The man swiveled his head so he could talk to his wife (girlfriend?) but his muscular torso continued to block the open doorway. He turned back to me: "We're going to eat, O.K.?"

"Later." The man shut the door.

I continued down the landing. Sometimes I knocked; sometimes I just waited expectantly outside a door as if trying to feel out the character of the people within. Most weren't home. Some called through the closed door that they were too busy to talk or they didn't want anything.

One man with a bushy mustache opened his door just as I was about to knock. He pushed by me quickly with a "Hi" and a friendly nod, and clattered down the stairs. As the man passed the manager's door, it opened and the Arnie, the manager came out. "Hi Al," Arnie said. "Hi Arnie," Al called as he disappeared from the courtyard.

Arnie remained outside. His head turned slowly in an arc around the courtyard as if searching for me hiding on the landing above. I shrank back in the shadows and held my breath. Then Arnie went back into his apartment.

A woman came to one of the doors, finally, in response to my knock. I talked to her, making up what I was going to say as I went along. "I'd love for you to meet my husband," she said after a pause. The couple stood in their doorway chatting with me for several minutes. "An awful lot of single girls do live here," they both acknowledged, though they didn't offer any suggestions. The man thought there was kind of a cute blond living back in the direction from which I'd come. When he said this, his wife, a brunette, gave him a long slow look. They didn't invite me inside.

At last, I risked crossing to the opposite side of the courtyard where I would be in full view of the manager's searching eyes. A small card table stood outside the manager's office with a deck of cards and three glasses sitting on it. I figured I had at most a quarter of an hour before the manager reappeared.

"I'm new to the building," I told the tall angular brunette who answered my next knock. For a while, we talked through her partially closed door. She shut the door completely for an instant while she fumbled with the chain, but reopened it again to invite me in.

"I'm a nurse," she said, after she'd brought two cups of coffee and a slice of cake to the table.

"I work as a computer programmer."

"That must be interesting."

"Not really, though it's fun at first."

The girl was not attractive, but her smile was warm and friendly. She was the friendliest person I'd met in LA, the only person I'd met really outside of work.

"Do you read your Bible?" she asked. Her question caught me off guard, uncertain what to answer. I must have nodded my head. "I've got one right here. We can read together."

She got up and fetched a very large Bible to the table. Her hips, I saw, were slim and unformed, their movement almost sexless, though she still carried the same warm smile that had first greeted me in the doorway. She can't have many friends either,

I thought, but I bet she's nice if you get to know her. I started to undress her in my mind.

"You don't believe in evolution, do you?" she asked.

"Yes, I do," I said, my mind still not on the conversation.

"That's not what the Bible says."

"Some of the things, the Bible says, I believe and some I don't."

"You've got to believe them all," she dictated. For a moment, I had a vision of myself in a long patriarchal beard, a Bible-bearing Christian with a thin, angular brunette wife trailed by three angular brunette daughters. Then I got up, downed the last of the cake in a single gulp and walked out of the room.

Outside in the darkness, the manager and his wife sat playing cards by the pool. They watched me as I walked back to my apartment, all the way around the U. I'd planned to knock on the door of the girl who lived in the apartment next to me, the one who said come back in half an hour, but with the pair of them listening downstairs, I just went back inside my apartment, turned on the stereo to drown out the Muzak, and went to bed. Eight-thirty in the evening. So much for life in LA.

Dansin

"I've an idea," says Iona Brown, "Let's go dancing."

Iona, a short stocky woman with long graying hair that reaches almost to her waist, has an erect carriage and a dignity that would be striking even in a suburban matron. Her dress is a simple smock that can easily be removed, washed, and worn again, but it flatters her figure and emphasizes the dignity of her carriage. You can sense she adopted the simple style long before she descended into poverty.

Her two friends, Margie and Sonja are more careless in their dress.

Margie clothes herself in clashing color combinations that always make those about her uneasy, even self-conscious. Today, for example, she wears a bright green scarf, a red silk blouse, and a skirt with black and white polka dots.

Sonja seems to have no pride in her dress at all, or perhaps it is simply a lack of caring and being cared for. Her clothes are soiled from the pavement on which she sleeps, and the food stains reveal the haphazard way in which she feeds herself. She wears the same clothes over and over, with no thought of a change, until her friends, Iona and Margie, concerned, force her, in the polite way women have, to change them: "Try this on, dear?" they say once they have led her to the secondhand shop or the mission, and while she tries the new dress on, they throw the old dress away.

Iona already knows what she will wear to the dance—a pair of black leather pumps, well hidden in the weeds near an abandoned oil well. One barely-visible scuffmark toward the heel of the right shoe soils their perfection. For Margie, the dance poses a problem: “It's country-western, ain't it. I got the dress, I think,”—(Margie has many dresses, skirts, and blouses all bundled together in the plastic shopping bags she carries with her everywhere)—”but I don't have the boots.”

“I got boot, see,” Sonja interjects.

Indeed, Sonja is wearing a pair of sturdy hiking boots with the Kelty label that were recycled through a local church by a member of the Sierra club.

“Yes, dear,” says Iona. She intends to see that Sonja's shoes are changed to something less outré before they go. But for Margie, she senses, nothing but a pair of authentic cowboy boots will do. “We must find you a pair of boots, dear.”

At the Salvation Army outlet, clerks can be persuaded to lower prices or even to give merchandise away; a token amount always changes hands, but frequently even this small amount will be supplied by the clerk in charge of the store. Alas, no cowboy boots are to be had though, as Sonja remarks, “plenty warm boots” are available.

A Deseret outlet is down the street, but this shop, too, is bootless. A secondhand shoppe and even a discount shoe store are visited before Margie suddenly remembers a church in Corona del Mar that never quite got around to holding a promised rummage sale. “I'm sure they got the boots I need; those people got class.”

Panhandling gets the three the bus fare to a few blocks from the Corona del Mar church and, when the rumors prove unfounded, a parishioner gives them a ride to another church in Newport where shoes must certainly be on hand. There are boots at this church, down in the basement, several boxes

worth and even some in Margie's size. But, "not quite what I'm looking for," Margie says in the end.
"What size are you?" asks the woman who gave them the lift. When Margie tells her, the woman says, "I wonder if my sister...?" She leaves them in mid-speech to make a phone call.

A fluttery matron who expresses equal amounts of charity and apprehension offers them a cup of instant coffee. Iona wonders, though she knows the answer, why charity is always accompanied by suspicion: in her experience, a charitable person may bend over backward to see the homeless get a meal, or a cup of coffee, or a pair of boots, but always at some remote neutral location and never in that same person's home.

When the Good Samaritan returns from telephoning her sister, she tells the three the boots and her sister will be there shortly. By the time the sister arrives, the matron who serves them tea and coffee is reduced to a nervous frazzle. She jumps up each time one of the homeless women rises from a chair, and follows them everywhere, even, as Margie observes, "to the bathroom."

The women, restrained and fretful in their chairs, respond to the sister's arrival like a kennel full of puppies freed at last for a run. But the best news is the boots are not only a perfect fit but, says Margie, "they are exactly what I wanted." She starts to step out of her skirt then and there, planning to exchange the soiled skirt for the one she will wear at the dance, when she is told, kindly but firmly, that there is a restroom where she might change.

"No, never in their homes," thinks Iona, but says aloud, "She's so pleased," bridging the awkward gap as they wait for Margie to return.

"I'm pleased too," says the Good Samaritan's sister, "To tell you the truth, I bought the boots originally because I wanted to take up country dancing and then my husband said he wasn't interested.

"Men," she adds scornfully and, at last, there is a topic on which all the women in the church, rich and poor, can agree.

Located on the main floor of a luxury hotel in Newport Beach, Duke's is a stone's throw from the tennis club where "Duke" Wayne himself once played; it is not intended to be, nor is it often, reached by public transportation, but, somehow, Iona discovered a bus stops just two blocks away. Transfers in hand, and only a few hours later, the three women walk up the palm-lined driveway to Duke's front entrance.

The dress code at Country-Western bars, even one so elegant as Duke's, has always been pretty much wear-what-you-look-good-in. The men go for jeans, long-sleeved shirts, and Stetsons, and almost all of them wear cowboy boots, but the women still tend to dress in whatever accentuates their best features or hides their worst. Some favor deep plunging necklines, some short, thigh-revealing skirts, and some schoolmarm gowns of the sort that cover the throat and reach clear down to the ankles.

The three homeless women, faces washed and hair brushed for the occasion, pass unnoticed.

Sonja stops a passing waitress, "drink," she says, "and two wawah." The voice is strained, rusty, but, undeniably, it is Sonja speaking.

"What kind of a drink?" asks the waitress.

"Gee, let's see," Iona begins, "It's been such a long time."

"Vrum," Sonja says, "Something with Vrum in it."

"We gotta special tonight," says the waitress, "Two for one on well drinks."

"Two vrum's" says Sonja immediately while the astonished Margie and Iona look on.

They are still more astonished when the drinks arrive. How many times have they been turned away unserved? Even waving a bill often is not enough. But these drinks are real and look cool and delicious on the waitress' tray. The drinks have to be paid for, of course. "Gaw mony?" Sonja asks, taking one of the glasses from the tray. Margie shakes her head. Thankfully, Iona has brought money.

"My God! Look who's over there by the buffet," Margie says, stealing a sip from Ionia's glass. "It's Pinkie."

"And look, they have a buffet," Iona replies cautiously, adding—almost as if were an afterthought—"Pinkie?"

"He's wearing a suit. Oh, doesn't he look good in a suit. You know Pinkie always was sweet on you, Iona."

"Yeah, well, I've never been that crazy about him," Iona replies, though the truth is she simply hasn't decided whether she likes Pinkie or not.

"Look who's with him, Paul and Arthur."

"They don't look as good."

"No, not at all."

"It's their clothes. They should have worn a suit or something. They should have fixed themselves up like Pinkie.

"Let's ask them to dance," Margie suggests.

"I've never asked a man to dance," Iona replies indignantly.

"Well, la-di-da. Who cares?" Margie says, "We came here to dance. Let's enjoy ourselves."

"Dans," Sonja echoes.

Iona is not unaware that Pinkie is attracted to her, has seen his frequent furtive glances as she walks along the sand. She has caught him watching when she goes for her shower in the morning, though he has not followed her, a gentleman, and looks away quickly if he encounters her nude by accident. He has had numerous awkward, barely believable excuses for standing near her, usually while she is talking with someone else. He has even said hello to her, what, half a dozen times, but he has never once had the courage to say, "Hi. I like you," or "Iona, would you go for a walk with me?"

Why can't he be a man and play the man's role?

She can sympathize, a little, with the blows his pride has suffered on his descent into poverty. But haven't they all suffered and in the same way?

Forced to flee from an abusive husband, Iona took to life in the open more like an animal released from a cage, than a prisoner condemned to poverty. Food was scarce on the outside, of course. And there were predators to contend with, but oh, my God, it was so much better than what she'd lived with before.

She loves the outdoor life, the strange calm after a storm, the shore clouds furious. Bothered early on by those about her, she found a stretch of beach that was hers alone, beneath the cliffs.

She slept there, made her toilet, and learned to make and enjoy the long walk to and from the pier in a daily search for food.

Once, an ugly, barrel-chested bearded man followed her to her home beneath the cliffs, took her, furiously protesting. She scratched at his eyes; he hit back, punching her in her stomach, and while she lay heaving, raped her.

She learned then about "free" clinics, about police indifference to crimes among the poor.

When the man followed her home again, she waded out into the surf. And when he snarled at her, "you'll have to come to the shore soon enough, bitch!" she simply swam away.

A youth, surfing alone in the moonlight, was amazed by the unexpected presence of a grandmother, like a mermaid, treading water inches from his board; they rode together into the beach close by the bright lights of the pier. She was wet from head to foot. But she merely disrobed, wrung out her dress, pulled it on again damp, and sat with the young surfer and his high school pals around a campfire till her dress had dried out completely.

Now, she has a dozen different places to call home. The place beneath the cliffs is still her favorite—she has purged her mind of all the hateful images, but she has a half dozen alternatives for when she must sleep, she must have shelter.

Pinkie. Pinkie! Why can't he also be a man and make the best of it?

Shit! She doesn't want to marry him; she just wants to dance. This time, when Pinkie gives her one of his furtive glances, she looks back eye-to-eye and waves. When he smiles, she walks over toward him, drink in hand.

Noon Run

(Adapted from the novel *San Onofre)*

." . . tired of waiting," her boss had said. Who cared if her boss were tired of waiting? Paula didn't need anyone to tell her what needed to be done or how to do it. The job would be done when the job was done. . . .

She was surprised to hear someone holler "Paula" behind her. Glancing over her shoulder, she saw Roxie jogging along with two other co-workers. "Sorry." Lost in her anger, she'd gone heels pounding by the others. Already, she was at the bottom of the hill, a half-mile gone without even thinking about it. Running was like that: if she thought about where she were going and how far she had to go then her chest hurt and she had to fight for every breath. If she just put her mind on something else, then it was like she were riding a horse, and the horse knew every step of the way and could gallop on forever over the fields and along the road.

Paula passed another small group from the mesa. Joggers, she thought disparagingly. They said they were runners, but what they did was jog. Paula ran: her body moved, legs kicking, arms swinging by her sides. Joyce should see her now. Joyce! She'd forgotten Joyce! Paula had been waiting for Joyce on top of the mesa, jogging in small circles in front of their building, when her anger over that morning's conversation with her boss had sent her blazing down the hill. She wondered if she'd run back up the hill so easily. Well, when you ran, you couldn't think about the challenges. You just had to run through them.

She was even with the plant parking lot now, lot 4, across the freeway, where she parked her car when she went down to the engineering building and the protected area. A quarter of a mile ahead, a lone figure kicked steadily down the road. The joggers and Joyce were somewhere behind Paula straining to catch up; but otherwise she was alone, with a warm sun, a blue cloudless sky, an occasional crack in the pavement, and her thoughts for company.

The runner ahead of her was a man. She could tell that much from the hips and shoulders, though she couldn't tell yet if she knew him. He had a short hair cut, blond or brown hair. Well, she'd catch up with him soon enough. The guano-spattered roof of Building One went by on her right with the sharp profiles of the two larger buildings coming up.

The gulls are circling, white and gray in pairs. Golden beaks. The sun is warm and golden.

She didn't seem to be gaining. Building Two and she could still only see the back of his head.

The road curved upward. Not enough to slow her down, but enough to keep her from pushing the pace on the runner ahead. Art thou fair Hermes, messenger of the Gods, who runs like the wind before me? As she got closer, she could see that his hair was not short, but had been gathered up in a rubber band and pinned behind him. And he was blond or reddish blond, not a brunette. A strong runner; this was her best day yet on the road and still he ran ahead of her.

My chest hurts. There is pain in my chest and the inside of my thighs. The warmth isn't enough; I feel pain. I cannot stop; I will run with the wind behind me.

They passed Building Three and she was still fifty yards behind. By then she had recognized the man. Mark Haines. It had to be Mark. Running the way everybody said he ran, effortlessly, untiringly. But she was gaining! Now, she was worried about going too fast. She didn't want to pass Mark, but she didn't want to put on the brakes.

Someone is close behind me: The new engineer who works with Unit One. Paula is her name.

She didn't want to have to pause as she came alongside him and loose her stride. She wanted to be running nice and easy. Now. A quick smile; he smiled back. He lost a step. She gained. He took two quick steps and then got back into her stride.

Can run as fast as me. We can run together.

They ran side by side, with only the sea on their right, and a single military vehicle, a jeep, stalled near them in the field. They ran together like the wind. She was sweating; they both were; the wind came off the ocean and touched them lightly as if one had barely caressed the other with a towel.

They ran into the open space where normally she turned back; a shunt road continued up the hill. Would he turn back here or go on ahead?

Purple and yellow flowers surrounded them. The clearing sat in a slight depression, hidden from the sea and the hills around. "What do you want to do?" Paula asked.

He put his arms on Paula's shoulders and his lips to hers. An electric tingle ran through her as their lips touched. *She tastes of oranges.* His body was close and comfortable against hers. They separated as the other runners came up over the rise, but turned back together and ran as one toward the mesa.

"Would you like to have dinner with me tonight?" he asked as they came opposite the plant again.

"Yes, I'd like that very much."

And they were both running tired, pushing their bodies, a temporary gear, while they waited for a second wind. When it came, they were at the bottom of the hill leading up to the mesa, and now they went pounding past the joggers returning, and there was Joyce just starting out (where had she been?), and then they were on the mesa, pushing for the final turn around the training building, running the last hundred yards side by side.

She couldn't resist kicking the last few steps, stopping just beyond where he'd stopped. When she turned to him, trying to speak, still not quite able to catch her breath, he said, as if putting a distance between them, "I've got to go in and change."

"Mark?" A question, a statement.

"I'll come by later to arrange a meeting place." He touched her arm lightly. She was still walking off her exhaustion, when he disappeared inside the building.

Shave and a Haircut

Pinkie's image in the mirror is distorted, partly as a result of a series of cracks that run the length of the glass. His hair is thick and matted, still black mostly, but with streaks of auburn where the sun has bleached it, and flecks of gray. He will brush his hair later, trying to restore its body, but he knows it will not look the same as it did only a few months before when he lived indoors. He needs a haircut, or at least a trim, but this, too, will have to wait. For tonight, he will just brush his hair, then plaster it down against his head with water and hope it will hold there while he dances.

Pinkie shaves himself carefully, trying to avoid even the tiniest nick, though it is hard to concentrate with half his attention focused on the door behind him. He is prepared to whirl and defend himself at the slightest suggestion of an intruder.

The clean-shaven part of Pinkie's face contrasts with the almost burnt red of his neck and shoulders. He frowns at his image, concentrating on forming a huge bushy moustache. As always, the moustache doesn't quite come up to his expectations. His sideburns, too, appear ragged and straggly, the results of the uneven cutting they received the last time he shaved.

The secret to a good shave, he thinks, is to get the face thoroughly wet beforehand and to wash the cheeks and the neck carefully with soap and hot water. It is not easy to get soap and hot water when one lives on the beach. But if he plans, if he waits the evening before until someone walks away from their fire without putting it out, and keeps the coals together, glowing brightly, until morning, why then he can start the fire up again and heat a can or two of water for a quick wash before he shaves.

He keeps a razor blade stashed in the restroom hidden in a crevice. The handle of the razor is in his pants pocket; he is afraid if the police find a blade in his possession, they will turn it into some sort of charge.

A sound comes from the doorway behind him, a footstep, the fluttering of a bird? He whirls, careful to lift the razor away from his face, holding it out and away from him like a weapon. There is nothing in the doorway. Nothing now. A soft coo tells him it had been a bird. I'm spooked, he thinks. I've been spooked for a long time.

He thinks about the dance and realizes he will not be able to put off the haircut. A trim, perhaps. He will have Bill trim his hair, though he cannot be sure of holding Bill's attention until the haircut is complete. Or perhaps he can persuade John the Barber to cut it. John is always eager to prove he was a barber once. Inevitably, John will lose his temper, perhaps at Pinkie for wiggling in the chair, perhaps at an innocent rusted trashcan perched upside down. He will begin to curse and swear in a language all his own and rave at unseen forms and attack them with his scissors.

Pinkie thinks back to a time when his ex would cut his hair, the erotic excitement when her hands would brush against his neck. And, before that, to a time when he would sit in a line of chairs with other men, while the barber trimmed and clipped and told stories to him and the other men around him.

After he is through shaving, Pinkie (what had been his name before? Jack? Ted?) lies down on the beach. The warm sun forms a pattern of green and brown dots on his closed eyelids. For a moment Pinky, too, is warm and loved. He would have lain this way for hours until jeering voices brought him to his feet, had not he had a sudden craving for a big breakfast.

He could get breakfast, a big one, at the Hourglass cafe, in return for an hour and a half, two at most of washing dishes. Sometimes during the week, if he is clean, they will feed him at the Hourglass even if they don't have anything for him to do. Breakfast at the Hourglass, some toast, a sausage, is something he can count on. Who needs lunch? And in the evenings, well, he will take what chance provides, maybe an old friend willing to spare a buck or two to buy him a meal, though he hadn't encountered an old friend in a long time, not one willing to recognize Pinkie (Ted) under all the dirt and hair and sand.

Tonight, he will have a magnificent meal, taking plate after plate from the buffet at one end of the dance floor. Sometimes, the hotel will provide two different sets of dishes. After the salads—bean and pasta and green leafy lettuce with whole cherry tomatoes, will come a second setting with meat and roasted potatoes and fresh-cooked green beans cut on the slant.

The Sunday evening buffet is something planned and part of Pinkie's week, now. Perhaps the only part of his life that is still planned.

He walks slowly across the parking lot that separates the beach from the highway, favoring his right leg where an open sore still bothers him. He hums as he walks, the same little tune he hummed while shaving, something remembered from the dance floor the week before. "The girl in the red dress." Or is it a girl in a red dress he danced with?

He stops humming when he hears a second tune, warm and clinging to his mind. The sound of a clarinet seems to come from all around him and, at the same time, to originate inside his head. Space music: Part electronic and part tapes of voices and musical instruments. Pinkie likes space music; sea music, really, for it is gentle and rhythmic like the sea. He likes space music but he doesn't like much of the other music he is forced to hear as picnickers and passersby rotate their boom boxes near his ear.

Pinkie remembers a conversation he had with Bill; they each had a beer and three or four hamburgers they rescued from a dumpster, and were talking about things they liked and didn't like about living on the beach. Bill told Pinkie the thing he hated most was having to listen to other people's music. Bill was sore about an almost-fight that had occurred earlier in the day; he had squared off against a bigger and more powerful man, while a group of the man's friends had jeered and egged Bill on.

The space music comes from a nearby camper trailer, a Star Fleet that belongs to old Julius. As always, Julius is sitting beside his camper reading a paperback western, his music pouring through the window behind him.

Parking at a State Park for more than three nights in a row is prohibited but, somehow, old Julius gets around this rule. The other retirees park for three nights at Tin Can then drive down the coast to spend three nights at Huntington Beach before driving back up the coast again. Julius might have driven up and down when he first moved to the beach, but now he spends all his days parked in the same spot, fishing and reading his paperbacks.

Julius likes a specific type of western, Zane Grey or Jack Schaefer, and he will read the same dog-eared paperback over and over. Pinkie knows better than to chide him for it. "I like reading the same book over and over;" Julius will say, "a man my age is entitled to read what he likes."

Sometimes, Julius disappears from the beach for days at a time. "I go to the mountains," he says, "I like the mountains."

Pinkie wants to say to Julius, "will you take me too?" but he's never quite gotten up the nerve. Pinkie isn't sure how he'd live in the mountains, where he'd get his food or whether it would be easy to find a place there to live. And, of course, there wouldn't be any Sunday dances in the mountains.

Julius looks up from his paperback and smiles at Pinkie. "Morning," he says, "you look happy today."

"Morning," Pinkie replies eagerly. "There's a dance tonight."

Julius puts down his book. "Of course, there is. It's Sunday. I see you've shaved for the dance."

Pinkie runs a hand over his cheeks, "How's it look?" he asks.

Julius considers the question, "You might want to shave a second time. Make it look super smooth," he adds thoughtfully as a look of panic crosses Pinkie's face. "And best get yourself a trim. Handsome man like you should take advantage of all his capabilities."

Pinkie smiles.

Julies continues, "Think you'll get yourself a hot one tonight?"

"I hope," says Pinkie. He remembers the dance in April when he picked up a thirty-four year old, or she picked up him. Four days in her apartment, lollygagging in her bathtub, experimenting with each of the myriad bottles and creams and aerosol sprays that she kept perched on a wooden shelf at the end of her tub, four days away from the beach, four days sleeping in a bed instead of on the sand, before she said to him, "Well, my boyfriend is coming back now."

"Got any advice?" Pinkie asks Julius, "I mean about getting a girl to come home with me."

"Naah. Women are your specialty. Ask me about fishing though and I'll tell you what to do." Julius looks Pinkie over carefully, still not too pleased with what he sees. "You'd do better to live on fish, Pinkie; keep you healthy. But no, you bums would rather prowl through dumpsters."

Not true, Pinkie thinks, and I'm not a bum. He likes fresh-caught fish, could eat fish day after day, pan-fried or burnt and crusty, straight out of the fire. He wears a fishing line now, tied round his waist like a belt. He needs another hook though; he lost the last of his cache of hooks to thieves the day before. God, he can taste that fish—the fresh white meat, the strong flavor of the pink flesh along the tail.

"I got to go," Pinkie says.

"Don't need to check in with me," Julius replies gruffly and turns back to his book as if Pinkie had never existed.

Pinkie is irritated and offended. And then he hears the words tossed back casually over Julius shoulder, spoken oh so quietly as if Julius doesn't care if anyone is listening or not, "Come see me, Pinkie, if you need another hook."

"Thanks Julius."

Pinkie's need for food leads him across the parking lot, along the sidewalk and, once he is has crossed the highway, past a line of surf shops displaying sandals and bikinis. Is Julius right about his luck with women? At times, he does think of himself as a gigolo, self-confident, knowing the two-step and the lambada, knowing what to say while he dances, knowing when to stop talking and persuading and listen to the woman. Then why am I so alone, Pinkie thinks, why am I so alone?

On the sidewalk outside Hoagie's Surplus, the proprietor is just setting out a series of wooden bins. Later in the day, these will be filled with items of clothing and labeled with signs that read "sale," "$s off," and "bargains." Pinkie shopped here once just a few weeks after he moved to the beach. His clothes had been stolen while he slept. He woke to find only a ragged pair of greasy pants riddled with holes in place of the clean shirt and worn sports pants he had used as a pillow. He wandered down the street dazed and stopped outside this same store to finger a pair of swimming trunks on sale. On the way to the fitting room, he was hailed by the proprietor, a swarthy Iranian, "Hey bum, where you going?"

"I'm going to try on these trunks, see if they fit."

"You got money?"

Hesitantly, Pinkie reached up to the cloth bag that hung about his neck. Still there! He took out two bills from the bag, unfolded them and showed them to the proprietor—almost enough to pay for the bathing suit. "I thought maybe you'd come down a little on the price," Pinkie said.

"Come down! You crazy, they already on sale. Besides, I take your money, you got nothing to eat." The proprietor looked him over carefully, "You push a broom, bum?"

"Sure," Pinkie replied, though he had not pushed a broom or a shovel since he was in his teens.

"You sweep out this place, I give you the suit. Only you still owe me. You got to come back tomorrow, sweep this place out again."

"Sure," said Pinkie, who would have been willing to sweep out the man's store for three or even four days in a row to get the suit.

The Iranian sent Pinkie to the Hourglass Cafe to work for his breakfast and, after the second day of sweeping was complete, gave Pinkie small amounts of money or articles of clothing out of the sale bin in return for odd jobs. Pinkie worked for the man for two or three weeks until one day someone else, perhaps it was one of the proprietor's many nephews, was put to work pushing broom in Pinkie's place.

At the Hourglass Cafe the proprietor and his wife greet Pinkie effusively and seem almost glad to see him. "Have I got my job?" Pinkie asks as they escort him back through the kitchen to the washing-up area behind. "You've got your job Pinkie," Max the proprietor says, smiling.

Pinkie enters his second home. He dons a clean white apron and begins the task of washing up. A stack of pots and frying pans is in one sink soaking in the steaming white suds; a stack of plates and glassware is in the other. He makes short work of the plates and has the sink empty just before the next stack arrives. The pots take longer; Chavez the cook always seems to be burning something, and Pinkie has to scrub out and polish each pot individually with a pad of steel wool.

Pinkie's hands and arms grow cleaner as he works; the hot water strips the outer layers of skin and leaves his hands fresh and pink. His arms lose their gray cast and are revealed bronzed and strong.

I used to work in an office, Pinkie thinks. My hands were always clean. I got a manicure once every two weeks. When I wanted a cup of coffee, I would ask Germaine or one of the other girls to fetch it for me.

When the breakfast crowd falls off finally, Pinkie sneaks off to the restroom. Carefully, he shuts and locks the door and, after relieving himself and scrubbing his hands once more, he takes off his shirt and begins to apply the liquid soap from the dispenser to his upper torso, using plenty of hand towels on the floor of the restroom to soak up the excess water. He slips off his underpants—they are caked with dirt, and puts them in the sink to soak in the hot water. There is barely enough time to run a wet hand towel around his groin, before they call to him through the door to come to breakfast.

Around two, Pinkie strolls back to the beach. He is well fed now; Max served the staff a huge platter of eggs and chopped ham before closing up the kitchen for the day. Pinkie feels almost clean. Only the sore on his leg and one raw area near his groin still chafe and bother him.

Pinkie compares himself with the other suburbanites heading to the beach for a day in the sun. His t-shirt is not much different from theirs—"Beach City" in orange letters above a blue ocean; but his pants, grease stained and slightly yellow around the crotch, are a dead give away. He is not dismayed. I got my dance clothes hidden, he rejoices.

Pinkie looks carefully about the restroom where he shaved that morning and, sure he is unobserved, withdraws a pair of toenail clippers from a crack in the wall beneath the sink. He leaves the restroom and walks slowly along the beach. Seated with his back to the surf, his eyes feast on bare skin, bikinis, sun block and suntan lotion while he carefully trims his nails in preparation for the dance, first his feet and then his hands. Finished, he heads back to the restroom and hides the clippers once more.

He looks in the mirror but is not pleased with what he sees. I'll shave again, he promises himself. And I'll find Bill or John the Barber to give me a haircut. I'll give myself a trim if I have to.

A shadow falls across the doorway as a slender figure, still more ragged then Pinky himself staggers into the restroom and walks over to the washbasin. The man throws up into the sink, then falls to the floor where, crawling on his hands and knees, he gradually makes his way out into the sunlight again.

Pinkie follows. He is sleepy and looks about for a quiet spot just above the high tide line where he can stay cool yet not be wet by the advancing tide.

"We sleep half our lives," Bill said to him once. "You mean one-third," Pinkie replied indulgently; Pinkie was conscious as always that he was better educated than most of the men he lived with on the beach. "I'm not talking about them," Bill replied, his emphasis on the "them," his head lifted disdainfully toward the houses perched high on the bluffs above, "I'm talking about us. We spend half our lives on the beach sleeping or trying to sleep or just resting because we're never ever really able to sleep for fear someone will steal our bedroll or drive his camper over us in the dark."

Bill told Pinkie this when Pinkie first moved to the beach, before Pinkie was willing to admit even to himself that the beach was where he lived. Pinkie hadn't quite understood what Bill meant then.

Before moving to the beach, Pinkie lived by himself in a small three-bedroom house, and before that he lived with his wife and two daughters. He had a job, well, a series of jobs, three years with this company, five years with that one. He wasn't one of those lifers, retiring with the same company he started with, ending his life in the company cafeteria eating with his daughters and maybe even his granddaughters. Not that staying with one company would have made any difference. There were men on the beach from Pennsylvania, and Ohio, and North Carolina who had worked all their lives for one company until that company laid them off or simply closed its doors.

Pinkie could have handled the punches. Something would have turned up. It always had turned up in the past, but this time there was the trouble with his ex, and a series of missed job interviews. And as someone, an employment counselor told him, it just wasn't the right time to be looking for work in Southern California.

Pinkie found the dance while searching for a replacement wife. He'd worked his way through the singles clubs from Parents Without Partners to Fun Loving Individuals Relating Together. FLIRT held a dance each Sunday in the Huntington Beach Inn just after their evening lecture. Pinkie attended their lectures—"You and the Power of Self," "Coping with Loneliness," and "Meeting the Ideal Mate"—but after awhile, he just went to the dances.

The FLIRT dance cost nothing to get in the door, and once in, Pinkie didn't have to buy a drink to stay. The waitresses would try to hustle him, of course: "Can I get you something, Sir?" they would say pointedly, when Pinkie was standing with a girl he was trying to impress. But generally, the dances were so well attended that he couldn't get hold of a waitress if he wanted to.

Sometimes there was no option but to buy the girl a drink, at which point he'd wave a credit card—which the waitress would not take—and stammer, "Looks like I came out without any cash." With luck, the girl he was trying to impress would pay for her own drink and offer to buy him one, too. Usually, he would refuse.

"Are you into health?" these women would ask admiringly. "I live at the beach," was his invariable reply, and most of the women nodded as if they understood.

With a hollow sigh he remembers her, not a particular woman but a composite of all the women he's made love to: a wife, a secretary just starting out on her first job, a mistress who'd been a June Taylor dancer, a cousin when he was sixteen, alone in her bedroom, her parents gone somewhere for the evening, expected later but back in time to discover them, and the middle-aged woman he'd stayed with the month before, who let him stay three days with her, remarking only once, the first day, on the ring in the bath tub, and again on the third day suggesting, no insisting, that he take a second bath.

He hadn't realized how much he had forgotten about personal hygiene. "But it's cold," he wanted to say to the woman but said nothing, realizing how difficult it would be to explain to someone who has never lived outside, what the fear of the cold can mean when there are no warm towels at hand, no walls to offer barriers to a cold, chilling wind.

Pinkie sits up abruptly, realizing he almost went to sleep, in fact, was asleep, still dressed in long pants, while all around him a crowd of sun worshippers—men in surf trunks and teeny-boppers in skimpy bathing suits, played on the sand.

Radios blare; two Marines, distinguished from the other bathers by their almost-skin-level brush cuts, toss a Frisbee back and forth between them; picnickers devour egg salad sandwiches and cherries and peaches, and finish with Zingers and a second can of Miller Lite.

A child runs past him, brandishing a small blue shovel. "Come back Clark," his mother cries. "Uh, uh," the child replies, shaking a maned head that seems disproportionately large for his small body. The mother runs into view, the deep cleavage in her halter virtually baring her breasts with each step. "Clark, you come back here," she says. Clark giggles and takes a few halting steps in mock flight before his mother sweeps him up into her arms.

About 4 p.m., Pinkie falls asleep, the sounds of the child and his parent still ringing in his ears.

He dreams a strange dream. He is standing by a railing overlooking the dance floor of a huge bar room with a western motif. A raucous party is in progress. On the bandstand, a female singer wails that her man is unfaithful, but the band drowns out her words. Men dressed in cowboy boots, jeans, and black Stetsons dance solemnly back and forth in a line. Pinkie thinks he recognizes the faces, though they are not of men he has known personally but of extras, walk-ons in some long-ago Western movie. The women at the dance, uniformly beautiful, wear short halter-tops that reveal bare breasts. Pinkie's own clothing, polished brown oxfords and a made-to-measure suit, seems terribly out of place. He had that particular suit custom-tailored in Hong Kong, several years before. "Every man should have at least one custom-tailored suit," he told his wife just after he booked the Crownfield order.

"Would you like to dance?" he asks the woman next to him. She laughs in reply, a loud, disparaging laugh. "Will you dance this dance with me?" he asks again. The woman and her friends laugh louder and louder until all the women in the room are laughing at Pinkie. He looks down. His suit is gone; he is wearing the same ragged clothes he was wearing at the beach, the dark stained trousers with the torn cuffs, the faded shirt with the missing buttons. I don't belong here, he thinks, and the people in his dream gradually clear a space around him.

He dreams another dream in which he floats gently on the sea; a porpoise nudges against him. And another dream in which Bill and John the Barber sit near him on the sand arguing. And another dream in which the last of the picnickers pack up their picnic baskets and their beach towels and walk away across the sand. A child throws a sandwich wrapper on the ground. "Billy you pick that up," his mother says.

When Pinkie's eyes open again, toward six, he is lying on his back, staring upward at the sky. He could be lying at home in a hammock. Or sleeping off the last of the beer at a company picnic. For a moment, he is uncertain where he is or what he is doing there.

Somehow he has moved closer to the trash barrel. A mound of sandwich wrappers and diet cola cans has grown around him while he slept. "My hair," he thinks, alarmed, and feels the top of his head. Not too sticky. He can wash it out in the saltwater shower near the restrooms. First, he will go into the ocean and get rid of the sand. Then, he will find the sliver of soap he has hidden away behind the brick and take his shower. He will trim his hair with a pair of almost dull scissors—there is no time for anything more—and, last, he will march proudly to where he has hidden his clean shirt and dress pants and put them on for the dance.

It took him months to find a place to store his clean clothes. The cracks in the retaining walls where he stores his razor and his by-now almost illegible driving license to hide them from thieves are too small. His main cache, where he keeps some mildewed clothing, is in the branches of a tree behind a long-abandoned billboard. This hiding place can be reached only by climbing to the billboard's elevated deck and then reaching around behind into the branches. Even this remote hiding place is not secure. One day when the gas company repaired a high-pressure line, the release of air sprayed a fine mist of oil all over his clothes. By the time he returned to make the discovery, the oil had penetrated deep into the fabric and could not be removed.

When Pinkie had his car, of course he stored all his belongings in it. He forgets exactly why the car was towed away. He was maybe a day or two late getting down to the pound to retrieve his car and by that time there were storage charges. He had to go borrow the money for the charges, hitchhiking back and forth from the station, and then there were more storage charges while he was gone. He told the men at the auto pound to sell the car and give him what money was left over. But they told him no, they had to wait until the storage charges exceeded a certain amount before they could seize the car for sale.

Finally, Pinkie found a junk dealer that was willing to give him $650 for a car that had once cost $13,000. He accepted apathetically, while behind his back the junk man gloated over the acquisition of a car worth several thousand dollars. Pinkie remembers the wise-ass clerk at the pound saying as the fine was paid, "but that's not your address, Mr. Williams, we know that's not your real address."

When the car was gone, he stored his clothes at a friends' house. But his friends didn't realize that when you hitchhiked somewhere you couldn't always show up at the exact time you arranged. So Pinkie would hitchhike maybe half a day up to the Valley, already feeling hot and tired, and when he got there his friends would be gone. He would wait outside their house and sleep on their back lawn until they got back or just forget the whole thing and return to the beach. "Take a bus," they said as if he had the money for a bus or as if there were a way you could take a bus to the Valley without first going into the City and then coming all the way back out again.

There were storage lockers, of course; he had some furniture in a storage locker; he'd paid for the locker six months ahead—when had that been? five, six months ago. But the storage place was closed on Sunday, so it wouldn't have done Pinkie much good to store his clothes there for the Sunday night dance.

He'd had to find a way to hide his clothes. Near the beach. Under a porch maybe. If he lived back east, he could hide his clothing under a porch, but you don't find basements or off-the-ground porches near the beach. The ground is too unstable. A cluster of apartments not far from the ocean had a set of lockers for their tenants. Not all of them were occupied. Pinkie thought about hiding his stuff in one of their lockers, but he'd heard too many horror stories about guys who came back to find their stuff gone and a new lock on the locker door. No, if he were going to hide his stuff in a locker, he would have to move in with it at night and take it away with him during the day in a bag or a shopping cart or something.

He remembered that warm day last March when he walked away from the cleaners with his one, his only, pair of dress slacks and a dress shirt, both neatly pressed and on hangers, wondering where am I going to hide these clothes? While he was walking, his worn shoes carrying him away from the beach—he wasn't going to walk toward the beach with those clean clothes all set out nice and neat on a hanger—he saw an open garage and an elderly man standing inside in the shadows, fumbling with a stack of newspapers. On impulse, Pinkie went up to the man and asked him if he could store his stuff there in the garage.

"Why don't you get a job?" the man replied though Pinkie hadn't asked him for money or anything. "I've got a job interview," Pinkie said, thinking this might be what the man wanted to hear, "next week." Pinkie smiled ingratiatingly at the man and went on talking—a good salesman always went on talking—"No point in my going on an interview if I don't have clean clothes to wear."

The man looked Pinkie up and down from Pinkie's unshaven face to his ripped shoes with their ragged laces. Pinkie waited, but the man didn't say anything, not a yes, not a no, just looked him up and down. "O.K.," the old man said, finally, "you can keep your clothes here. Just knock up at the house when you want them. I don't want you wandering around down here in the garage. Might have to shoot you or something."

Pinkie came back to the man's house Sunday after Sunday after that, once on a Tuesday when he did have a job interview—they said he was overqualified, and every Sunday evening about an hour or two before the dance. The man never said anything about it being Sunday and it not being very likely that Pinkie had a job interview that day.

When Pinkie reaches the man's house—Ed is the man's name—he is surprised to find the tiny yard surrounded by people. Pinkie hasn't been concentrating on where he is going, for his feet know the way, and his sudden arrival at Ed's house surprises him. An ambulance pulls away from the curb and a second vehicle, an ancient blue Ford driven by a blond woman—Ed's wife, he wonders—races off to follow it.

"What happened?" Pinkie asks no one in particular. No one replies. Pinkie walks up to one man, an older fellow with stained gray pants who doesn't look any more prosperous than Pinkie himself, and addresses him directly. "What happened?" he asks a second time.

"Guy had a heart attack," the man replies.

"Ed?" Pinkie asks, "Was it Ed?"

"Guy who lives here," is the laconic reply.

"How'm I going to get my suit?" Pinkie says to himself and then feels guilty for saying it; he should be worrying about Ed instead; Ed is such a nice guy. But Pinkie can't bring a halt to the sick feeling that is gnawing away inside of him: If I can't get my suit, I can't go to the dance.

Pinkie walks around the house looking for a doorway. He is brought up short on one side by tall wooden fence that blocks off the back yard. A small door on the other side of the house leads into the garage. Pinkie tries this door, shaking the handle; it is locked.

He walks around to the front of the garage and stands on tiptoe to peer in through the window. Is that his suit hanging in the back by the water heater? Maybe... maybe he could take a brick.

He remembers the first time he came to Ed's garage to pick up his clothes. He went up to the house like Ed asked him to and waited a long time for first Ed's wife and then Ed himself to come and answer the bell. Ed gave Pinkie a nod that might have meant anything and then disappeared inside the house. The next sound Pinkie heard was that of the garage door lifting. He dashed down the steps and around the corner of the house like a dog hearing the arrival of his master's car. When he did not spot his slacks and shirt, he raced all around the garage looking for them, before Ed showed him where his clothes had been carefully put away inside a suit bag. "Thanks Ed," he says out loud now as part of a prayer for Ed's recovery, even though running through Pinkie's head, over and over, is the constant refrain, "how am I going to get my slacks?" "How am I going to get my slacks?"

Pinkie walks along the beach path, his head bowed despondently. It has grown dark gradually and one by one the lights have come on along the highway and in the buildings opposite. For one moment he stands erect and looks across toward the motel where people are already beginning to walk up the long ramp to the dance. "I'm going to get my slacks," he says determined.

Across the street from Ed's house, a group of young people sits outside in lawn chairs, beer cans at their feet. A cigarette glows briefly and then winks out. Pinkie walks along the edge of Ed's driveway looking for a brick or a stone he can use to break a window. He reaches down for the handle of the garage door and tugs. The door lifts! It is unlocked. Stunned, he walks back carefully into the darkness, edging around Ed's car—he'll never drive this old car again, Pinkie thinks—his hands outstretched before him. He is standing by the water heater, his hands on the suit bag, when the lights go on.

"Stop right there." A short female figure, that of Ed's grown daughter, stands framed in the kitchen doorway not more than a few yards from where Pinkie stands. At first, he thinks she's just a kid, but then he sees the lines around the eyes and mouth. Maybe 34, but maybe 44. Very attractive, pretty hair, a full bosom. She is short, no more than 5'4" or 5'5," and ought not to have frightened him, but her mouth and face are set in determined lines. She holds a small target pistol in her outstretched hands. "I wasn't stealing anything," Pinkie says, "I came to get my pants."

"Your pants?" the woman questions. Her full lips curve scornfully.

"My pants and my shirt, Ed lets me keep em here, in the bag," Pinkie gestures with his hands. "Let me show you ma'am." He reaches out.

"You keep your hands on the car," the woman snaps and brings up the pistol.

"Yes ma'am." Pinkie is trembling all over and at the same time he is thinking how beautiful she is. Ed's daughter appears to be thinking about him too though not with the same passionate intent. She studies his ragged figure as if examining some new specimen under a microscope and, for an instant, Pinkie sees Ed's intent features superimposed on hers.

She gestures with the pistol a second time, "Open the bag," she says. Pinkie opens the bag and shows her the pants and the shirt. "My size see. I keep em here so they won't get stolen."

The woman restrains a smile. She lowers the pistol and Pinkie no longer feels afraid, though he is still uncertain what she is going to do about his clothes. "I guess those are your clothes all right," she says, still smiling, "OK, you can take them."

"Can I put them on here?" he asks. She laughs and nods yes. But when she does not move he adds, "And could I have some privacy?"

"Of course," she says, and retreats into the kitchen. He takes off his sweat-stained garments quickly and lays them across the car top; then he carefully removes his pants and shirt from the suit bag. The pants crease is still sharp and the shirt, although beginning to look somewhat gray around the collar, is still good for another evening's wear.

"Can I bring 'em back afterwards," he says daringly once he is dressed, "I mean if I don't meet someone."

"Your clothes you mean? Yes you can." She bursts into deep full-throated laughter. "What's your name?" she asks.

"Pinkie. I mean that's not my name, that's what they call me."

"What do you call yourself? I mean what did your mother call you?" she asks when he hesitates in replying to her first question.

"Ted, Ted Williams, like the ball player."

"Or like Ed my dad." Does she look shocked or is she laughing? At him or with him? It is important that he understand women.

"Would you like some water?" she asks.

"Yes ma'am."

"You're going to the dance aren't you?" she asks as she fills the glass, "The FLIRT dance at the Huntington Shores?"

"Ye..., yes," Pinkie confesses. He feels sheepish, awkward in her cool presence. Looking down at his pants, he absently smoothes their crease. For a moment, he wonders if the quick haircut, the morning shave were enough.

"You look fine," she says, as if reading his mind, "quite handsome. I go to the FLIRT dance myself sometimes. No, don't worry," she adds when she sees his reaction," I won't tell anyone. I may even dance with you."

She takes his hand and shakes it. Her hand is so tiny. Her skin feels so smooth. "You can bring the clothes back afterwards, OK."

"Tha-tha-thank you. I just hang them on the handle."

"K. I'll put them away for you."

Pinkie stands in the hotel's parking lot well back in the shadows near a line of parked cars and watches as one by one, and only occasionally in twos or threes, people begin to move up the ramp and into the hotel.

At first, no one at all drives into the hotel lot and he felt a surge of panic. Has the dance been cancelled? Then with relief, he notices first a few men, their jackets faded, and then one or two women, the latter seemingly a bit uneasy, move toward and past him into the motel.

The men arrive singly, taking a deep breath and squaring their shoulders before moving decisively up the ramp. The occasional woman arrives alone, doing her best to remain inconspicuous as she sidles past him toward the hotel, but most of the women come with a hunting partner or in a group of three or four.

A car pulls into the lot and moves slowly forward, its driver peering through the fine mist searching for a vacant space. A door opens; a pause while the car's occupant checks her hair and the line of her dress in the car mirror, and then, one hand holding down the edge of her skirt, she slides across the seat and out onto the asphalt.

An older woman, hips swaying, walks forward along the line of motel doors. The movement of the hips changes as he watches; they roll slightly then oscillate from side to side as if their owner were deliberately controlling and optimizing their motion. By the time the woman reaches the front of the motel, the hips are fully under control.

Two women just ahead of him teeter on their high heels like schoolgirls trying on their mothers' clothing. The shorter of the two wears a fur coat, earrings and a carefully tailored pants suit. Despite the elegance and care with which she has dressed herself, Pinkie senses she is nervous and ill at ease. Her friend urges her forward. She hangs back. "Am I beautiful enough?" she seems to be saying to herself. She is the one for me, Pinkie thinks.

He follows, trying to blend with them, and when one of the women smiles, though she is not the one he has been watching, he smiles back and starts a conversation. He moves up and alongside her.

Earlier, when he thought ahead to the dance, he planned to keep track of every movement, color, sound, storehousing memories to comfort him later. But now his plans fall apart. One instant he is walking along the motel hallway, the next he is standing by the dance floor.

A rush of sound, of color overwhelms his senses, gradually resolving into couples on the dance floor, two men standing near him against the wall talking, glasses in their hands, and a waiter who brushes past him with gleaming plates of fragrant steaming food for the buffet.

One moment Pinkie is out in the parking lot, watching in the shadows and then ...

He is inside.
He is talking.
He is dancing.

He is somebody again.

Three Things One Needs to Do in a New Town
(adapted from the novel, *Sad and Angry Man)*

He picked up his new life partner as casually as you or I would rent a DVD. Or did she acquire him?

There are three things one needs to do in a new town, that is, once one finds a place to live. Locate a market convenient to the new apartment, have the electricity and gas switched on, and get a telephone installed.

The phone company told him he'd have to wait three weeks before they could install a phone. This being well before the days of the cellular, his only option was an answering service.

He got a fist full of quarters and established himself in a phone booth with a ballpoint, a stack of dimes and the yellow pages. Two stacks of quarters later, the margins of the phone book were covered with prices. Each service had its own method of billing, its own complicated set of options. He could have flipped a coin. Instead, he did what he always did in these situations and opted for the service with the friendliest receptionist.

The short blond woman who welcomed him to Ansa-Pine, seemed somewhat vague about the details. "You'll have to ask Joann," she kept repeating in slow, almost dull-witted fashion.

"And what's your name?" he asked, hoping this might put her at her ease.
"Peri." Her strong rural accent induced a strange set of conflicting emotions. Her face was so right for him, her accent and her mannerisms were so wrong.

"My name is Phillip."

"You're not from around here."

"I just got to town."

She gazed at him intently as if searching for the content of his character. He gazed back. Undeniably attractive, though a far cry from any women he'd dated. Small firm breasts, held proudly almost arrogantly, and a narrow waist that flared out at the hips; short, tiny-boned, almost frail, with a way of cocking her head on one side like a bird as she talked. She didn't appear to be wearing any makeup, and didn't need it, he thought. Her eyes were a lively blue, somewhat careworn. Her hair was a sort of dishwater blond with a perm that hadn't quite taken; stray locks would uncurl suddenly and fall forward across her face; she pushed them back with her tiny fingers, but they always fell forward again.

To get a date with a girl, you first have to ask her. "You are very beautiful," he said.

"Are you a doctor?" she asked ignoring his words.

"A doctor? Why do you think that?"

"The way you talk."

Her last word, "talk," was drawled, impossibly long. For an instant, he thought she might be making fun of him. Weren't city slickers always fair game? "Not exactly a doctor," he replied, "But I have a Ph.D. I'm an administrator."

"That's nice." This seemed a woefully inadequate reply, almost a put down, yet when Joann returned, "He's a Ph.D.," were the first words out of her lips.

Joann was all business: "Were there any questions she might answer?" But he'd already made his decision. "I'll buy the service. And is it all right if I take your secretary to lunch?"

Peri gave him a strange look. "You haven't asked me yet."

He smiled at her. "Will you go to lunch with me?"

At lunch—Joann had taken only a few minutes to get the details of billing and payment arranged—he repeated that he'd just arrived in town. "You could live with me," Peri said, "Can you pay your share of the rent?"

He said he could pay both their shares.

She gave him another of those penetrating stares. "You're pretty forward."

"You're pretty attractive," he replied.

She snorted, not exactly overawed. "Well, there are two bedrooms. My girlfriend just moved out. Maybe for now, you could sleep in one of the bedrooms and I could sleep in the other."

He didn't say any of a half dozen not-so-clever things that came to mind. He was satisfied just to be near this attractive, engaging woman.

Peri seemed quite casual about giving her house key to an almost total stranger. He telephoned her anyway as soon as he unloaded his car, both to reassure her he was going ahead with the plan and to ask for her suggestions for a dry cleaner.

Directions in hand, he headed out almost immediately from the small two-bedroom cottage in which she lived, first to the grocery store—he would try to buy his own stuff and not impose—and then to drop his suits and dress pants off at the cleaners. His suits had not done well in his automobile trunk; they'd started out on top, but had gradually worked their way toward the bottom as a result of a series of after-dark retrievals.

The supermarket was fascinating, new smells, new products. He tended to linger in grocery stores, inherited from his mother, to look at each of the fruits and vegetables as if seeing them for the first time. He bought beets, lettuce, parsnips, and green peppers. And a bag of squishy boiled peanuts, from a vendor on the sidewalk outside the store. He also bought strawberries and a fresh pineapple from which the outer husk had been removed. Moving-in gifts for her.

When he emerged from the supermarket, raindrops spattered from the pavement and awnings. Not a cool rain, but a warm one that only made him feel hotter and stickier.

Suddenly, he realized he was afraid to go back to Peri's cottage, scared that barriers would suddenly appear, his key would not fit, the girlfriend who had moved out would return to displace him, or Peri herself would reappear and say, "I'm sorry but I've changed my mind."

He pushed through the rain and fear, and then, miracle of miracles, the door opened to his key, there was no waiting message of dismissal, and the sky cleared long enough for him to move the groceries and the last few remaining items from his car.

He had offered and was looking forward to taking Peri out to dinner, but she surprised and pleased him by offering to cook for them both. "I don't cook often," she said, "living alone and all. That's why I'm just skin and bone. I'd like to cook for you, for the two of us."

"Thank you."

"How's the room?" she asked changing the subject, abruptly. He hoped he would soon adapt to the way her mind leaped from topic to topic.

"Quite large," he said, "I'm going to go looking for a bed tomorrow. Oh, and do you have an extra book shelf?"

"There's no bed?" she repeated, fixing on the first thing he had told her. She sounded surprised.

"No. The room's pretty bare; maybe that's why it looks so large." He laughed nervously.

"She was supposed to leave the bed. My girlfriend," she continued, when he looked puzzled.

"No. No bed. I can sleep on the couch." He pointed to the piece of furniture in question, though he was actually planning to sleep on the floor.

"Best eat." she said tersely, putting the problem aside. Dinner was ready. Peri had used the vegetables he bought that afternoon, though she surprised him by keeping the greens he would have discarded and cooking and serving these separately. With the addition of some ham and biscuits, homemade ones, not the heat-and-serve-in-a-tin kind he always bought, they had a wonderful meal. "I really like strawberries," she said, and she whipped up some cream she found in the back of the refrigerator—"my girlfriend's"—to put on top.

Bedtime was awkward. At the last moment, Peri suggested he sleep in her bedroom, each on their own side of the bed. "Can you be trusted?" she asked.

He looked perplexed.

"If I let you sleep next to me, will you stay on your side of the bed?"

"Yes. I suppose. Yes, of course."

He didn't volunteer a second time to sleep out in the living room. He wanted to be next to her. It would still be fun even if he lay awake all night.

He slept though, immediately and deeply. Who wouldn't after waking at six a.m. for a final cross-country dash, driving in the rain, along a backcountry road, finding a cottage, unpacking the car. . . .

In the middle of the night, it began to rain again. He woke, went to the toilet to urinate, then carefully slipped back in bed beside Peri. What would happen, he wondered, if he were to try to make love to her? Her back was to him, his nose buried in her hair, and he slipped his arms around her, his hands on her breasts, cuddling her rump with his loins, two spoons in a drawer. Her hair smelled of seaweed, the smell of the sea. He heard the rain falling; he felt tremendously grateful she'd not moved when he'd touched her, but had left her small firm breasts in his hands, her nipples pressing out against his fingers.

When he woke again, it had stopped raining. The air in the room was unexpectedly cool. He shivered, reached for his shirt and put it on over his shoulders, leaving the chest unbuttoned.

Peri was turned toward him, her face as calm and peaceful as the face of a sleeping child; a slight hint of moisture gave her cheeks a sheen that glowed in the pre-dawn light. Without thinking, he reached out and clasped her to him in a thoroughly fatherly hug. And then—there was no denying it, her loins began to grind against his. "Peri?" he whispered softly; he heard no reply; she might still be asleep. Asleep or awake, the movements of her hips continued, until there was no way he could conceal his own rising excitement. When had she taken off her panties? Hadn't she had them on when they first slipped in bed together? "Peri?" She sighed, reached up and kissed him lightly on the lips. He kissed her back and then, as easily if they had been making love all of their lives, he slipped inside her, and was clutched by arms, hands, and fragrant womb.

Part II: One-Night Stands

The Wrong Kind of Music

He'd opened her bedroom window, Diana discovered. She could hear the cars whizzing by on the rain-slicked street outside.

"Is that all right?" he called from the bathroom.

"I love fresh air," she lied cheerfully.

"Reminds me of the theme from The Bodyguard," he said, stepping out of the bathroom, toweling himself dry.

"Pardon me?" She looked him over carefully, surprising herself by her lack of embarrassment. Flat stomach, smooth skin, every bit as adorable as when she'd first seen him dancing earlier that evening.

"The song. I had this other girl friend once. We'd come home from a date and were making out on the couch, you know, like the two of us were a few minutes ago. This schmaltzy song was playing on this old radio she had, a big wooden monster left over from the '60s, something about eternal love. I asked her what the song was."

"The theme from The Bodyguard," Diana said, turning from where she'd been hanging up his pants and shirt in her closet, "I haven't heard it in years."

"I hadn't heard it at all. Must have been on top 40. She asked me what kind of music I listened to."

"What kind of music do you listen to?" Diana asked, trying to draw him into the here and now.

He sidestepped her question and looked around the room.

"I need the shirt." Taking it from the closet where Diana had hung it up, he let his towel slip, uncared for, to the floor. "Just to cover my shoulders. Anyhow, I came into the kitchen the next morning for breakfast and she's got my station playing on the radio. Same thing when I saw her again that evening."

I'm really not interested, Diana thought as she studied the towel. Why do you imagine I want to hear about your last conquest? Talk to me. Talk to me the way you were talking to me downstairs, about how beautiful I am, how you like my laugh, how you want to spend the night clinging to my breasts.

She'd been taken instantly by his voice, deep, warm, resonant. Now, it just droned on.

"We pretty much spent every night of those first weeks by ourselves, weekends dancing, weekdays cuddling while she worked on her lesson plans—her students were a grade ahead of yours, by the way, fourth instead of third. "Then, one day, she announces she'd like to give a dinner party, make use of all those fancy recipes of hers. I ask what I can do to help, and she tells me not to worry, she has everything under control. Put me off a little."

He'd put his shirt back on, and slipped under the covers as cool as you please. I guess that means he's spending the night with me, Diana thought inanely.

"You start spending weeks together with one person and you begin to think you and that person are one. Not this time. I show up on the afternoon of the party, a Friday I think, with a bouquet of flowers and she puts them aside, not even in water, because they don't fit into her decor or something. I'd come early, figuring we might mess around before dinner, but, no, she's got plans for that time, too. Long warm bath, hour and a half putting on her dress.

"It's a great meal—I'll give her credit for that—but I'm bummed because I'm not part of it. Part of the decor maybe, along with the pewter candlesticks and the damask tablecloth, but not part of her household, not the significant other I'd imagined myself to be.

"The guests who rate all this fuss consist of a single couple, John-somebody, who she works with and is always talking about, and his wife. My girl and John talk continuously, about work mainly, while John's wife pouts, looking as left out and upset as I feel.

"I make one nasty comment—about the string beans being canned, not fresh, and, well, I fall asleep after dinner. She isn't pleased. We're in the bedroom—God, we even make love, and she says she's sorry, she doesn't think it's going to work out. I put my clothes back on, check my hair in the mirror, and when I come out, the radio is back on her station, W A V E, the Waaaave, with Kenny G and Whitney Houston to see me to the door."

Diana crossed to the closet as he finished his sentence and took out the pants and shirt she'd just put away. Now, she held them out to him.

"I hope you won't be too upset," she said, "But I seem to be coming down with something. It probably would be best if you didn't spend the night here after all."

As he clumped angrily down the stairs, she closed her bedroom window, shutting out the noise.

Memoir:
Two Girls, One Night in Hawaii

Like Charlie Brown, I knew a little red-haired girl in the first grade. I pushed her off the sidewalk, threw sand in her hair. And thereby launched the most successful career as a beach-boy since Erik Estrada.

Actually, it took me somewhat longer to learn to meet girls. A lot longer. Say, four years at college and three years at Missiles and Space. Then I got laid off by the company and got the chance to put what I'd learned into practice.

Lesson 1 (Nancy's rule): *If you want a date with a girl, the first thing you must do is to ask her.* I asked the girl behind the counter, judging her a nine. She was Italian or a little Italian, full breasted on a small frame, long hair, lots of makeup, long eyelashes, long, sharp fingernails. "I like your hands," I said. "Tell me your name: Your name, your phone number. Give me a chance to call you when I know something's happening."

(See the way I come on? Strong, forceful, in control.)

"Something's happening?" she replied, her voice like honey on macadamia-nut pancakes. She was alive and paying attention to me. (How do these things work? Why is meeting people such an art?)

"I'd take you to coffee," I babbled, "If I knew where they served the best coffee in Honolulu. I'd take you to Lums and buy you a beer if it was two in the morning and we were on the mainland. But I... I'm Haole here.

Lesson 2: *Keep Talking*. It's not what you say that's important. It's that you pay attention to the one you're with."

My girl-—the Italian, was paying attention to me. (Or was she cracking up, laughing.) Maybe she thought I was some kind of nut. Maybe she thought I was the greatest. The important thing was she was talking to me, no longer a fantasy, thinking it over.

"Haole. You're new." she said thoughtfully. (She knew I knew she was thinking it over. She looked me up and down while she thought.)

"Haole, there's a place a lot of people go to. Called the Green Lobster. Beer, pretzels, everybody sings along with the band. If you like that sort of thing?"

The sort of thing I like is a rich full mouth, long sharp fingernails, and a set of big, full breasts, preferably pointing in different directions. Beer parlors are O.K. for celebrating after an exam or a liftoff. But they're noisy, the bandsmen are raunchy, the sawdust is there just to cover the beer the waiters spill.

Be positive: that's Lesson Three. Girls like men that know how to have fun. Beer parlors are pretty neat places. So much is going on, you don't need to make conversation, just sit and wink and drink.

Afterward, she took me home like all good island girls in the storybooks. She stayed home from work the next couple of days with a 'cold', and when we weren't making love in her apartment, we'd be parked somewhere high above the surf making love in her car. If we weren't doing it in the back seat, her long perfect fingers would be inside my fly, tugging and caressing, getting me ready for action again.

Girl liked variety; she liked me in her mouth, and she liked me between her legs. Sometimes, we'd do both, alternating back and forth until I no longer had any control and came violently inside her or against the seat. But seven days of lovemaking, seven days and six nights, were all my Hawaiian tour allowed. "Girl," I said, "I've got to get back on the tour."

"You told me you were new," she said, sounding betrayed, "You said you came here to look for a job and settle down."

I explained about the tour, the seven days and six nights in Hawaii by the grace of InterCosmopolitan and their low, low all-inclusive fares. I told her about the bus that took you around to all the sights, then brought you back to your hotel again.

"You kind of got off the tour," she said. She no longer sounded disappointed and unwilling to understand. And she let her fingers do the walking down my thigh.

I had gotten off the tour at the very first opportunity. The let downs began in the Los Angeles airport with each glimpse of my gaggle of fellow tourists: A collection of turkeys and turkeyettes from the first spinster schoolteacher to the final candidate for 'Miss Mouse'. The Bon Voyage party—another of the fabled attractions of 'Club InterCosmopolitan,' sagged rather than sparkled.

The 'Club' was a gimmick. A five-buck membership included in the tour price allowed InterCosmo to book us all at a reduced rate—at least, that's what the salesperson told me. Whatever, it wasn't such a bad deal for them or me. And a Hawaiian tour had seemed a hell of a good way to pass the time till I got another job. (O.K., so there isn't any prospect of my getting another job until our country has its next war.)

Lesson 4: *If it looks too good to be true, grab it!*

My island girl believed in coming before going. I don't know why I left her. I was in the twenty-fourth week of my unemployment insurance, the next to last week. I would have been better off to stay in Hawaii, forget the unemployment checks and start over. Instead, I took the next bus to the airport, alone. I had a bag I'd kept with me, and the hope that, somehow, InterCosmo had been shifting the rest of my luggage from hotel to hotel along with the tour.

Lesson 5: *Never pack more than you can carry with you.*

Mr. Drake, aging lavender director of InterCosmo, was not there to greet me at the ticket counter. Instead, a brusque voice, "I'm sorry Sir. You'll have to talk with the passenger agent."

The passenger agent smiled a lot. "We aren't able to accept these tickets, I'm afraid (smile). Your agency was in error in selling them. You may be able to get your money back (smile) when you return to the Mainland. Though I hear they've gone out of business (smile)."

"What about the tour! the hotels?! my luggage? What about the other people on the tour?"

"I suggest you do as they did several days ago, Sir. Buy a ticket for your return flight and arrange for alternative accommodations till then (no smile)."

"How! With my unemployment check?!"

"That's really not the airline's affair. Is it, Sir? If you wish, we might . . ." he began. But I'd stalked away.

Two of the mice from the tour were waving to me from across the airport terminal. The brown-haired one was a clinger, the touch of her twig-like fingers a prelude to a nasal monotone. She clung now to the hairy arm of her constant companion, a dark-haired plump Sicilian girl with her own form of speech impediment. Were they school teachers? librarians? social workers? They'd tried to sit next to me, to Grandfather Barnes, even to Mr. Drake, a determined homosexual if ever there was one. "Bon voyage," I'd wished them as I fled the tours, and now...

"We're all together again," said Miss Mouse.

"You're back!" black-hair brayed.

"What about our tickets?" I raged.

"Oh, we're going to stay another two weeks," mousy brown giggled. "We're...," she mumbled, "Would you like to ...?"

"NO!" I shouted, already strides away. "No," I said to myself, "no, no, no."

Back to the airport bus. Fare 45 cents. Cash on hand, 47 cents. Resources: one travelers check for twenty dollars; one poncho—army surplus; one tote bag containing razor, bathing suit, condoms. And waiting in the heart of the San Fernando Valley, just outside beautiful downtown Burbank, three unemployment checks that had to be signed and countersigned in person.

Lesson 6: *You can't rekindle an old flame.* You. . . I was too angry to put my feelings into words. I stood outside her window, waiting in the rain. My Island beauty was inside, warm and comfortable. The cries coming from her window were familiar. But someone else was inside her.

I undressed on her porch and hung my suit on a hanger that had held my poncho. I hung my last dress shirt under the suit. I put on my bathing suit, my Primo sports shirt, and the poncho. I left the suit and the dress shirt along with a note—"Please have this suit cleaned and pressed by Friday." Then I walked away. It took a lot of walking. It was morning before I reached the coast, noon before a series of rides brought me to the cliffs at the edge of the Waipio valley. The Waipio was a deep cleft in the volcanic rock, "a descent into the primitive," according to the guidebook. I remember the view at the valley's edge, vividly. It is still as real to me as the long night of rain when I lay huddled in my poncho and the flood that drove me out.

Far, far below was a narrow alluvial plane, the river running to the sea, and the black volcanic beach. A jeep trail marked '4 wheel vehicles only' wound down the cliff. Across the beach, a second great slab of stone sealed off the valley. Both cliffs reached far out into the sea with no prospect of escape.

The jeep trail disappeared into a low cloud. Sometimes as I walked, I could see across the valley—the lush rain forests, like hanging gardens, the silver green of the Koa, the dark green of the Maile tree. And sometimes, I could see nothing at all in the mists. As I rounded an outside curve, the wind tore at my shoulders. Far below were the sea sands, jet black beneath the surf. Far off in the stiff shore breeze, the cold waves dashed on the rocks, a sound like wooden ships breaking and the screams of children. The mist was cold and damp; it swallowed the sounds and light and everything I remembered.

I could see only the trail itself, the small signs of animal life, the ferns and the vines that led the way back up the hillside. The pig persimmons, a type of shrub, bore a small green fruit about the size of my fist. They were tasty, but the juicy pulp was filled with seeds. The same seeds lay untouched in the lumps of animal feces that dotted the trail.

Guava grew near the path too, both sweet and sour guava, and papaya, and granddaddy cocoanuts. I have eaten the green cocoanuts they sell at Waikiki, with the juice still spicy and effervescent, and the stale cocoanuts they sell in the grocery stores on the mainland, but these granddaddies were a third, entirely different fruit. Ripe of its own accord, inside each shriveled husk juice and pulp had merged into a gigantic ball of toasted cocoanut candy.

Within the valley, the trail paralleled the river, a broad, deep stream that divided the valley in two. The river had numerous branches that surrounded and filled the farm patches of taro and rice. A farmhouse could occasionally be glimpsed in the mist. Each time the trail split, I chose the branch that kept me furthest away from the signs of civilization.

A dog had followed me down through the mists. He raced in and out of the underbrush, though he preferred a trailing position about ten paces behind me. Whenever I looked back, the dog was crouched, head up, as if to say, "Can I come?" And I always jerked my head forward to reply, "Onward, man and dog."

The river was not impassible, as I'd imagined in my first glimpse from the cliffs above. It grew shallower as it branched and subdivided. I took off my shoes and waded each time the trail crossed or merged with a stream. After awhile I discarded my trousers. They were too wet and too encumbering.

By evening, I found a relatively dry patch of ground on which to camp, and proceeded to gather a small supply of guava and granddaddy cocoanuts. Nightfall was abrupt and terrifying, ending in an all-enveloping darkness. Although it was only seven or eight in the evening, I lay down on the ground in my poncho and tried to sleep. I dreamt of parking in the hills above

Los Angeles, someone next to me on the seat, and the lights of the city below. I slept in fits and starts, waking each time to that terrifying blackness. (My dog slept near me in the darkness. I could hear him breathing, but I could not see him.)

The next day it began to rain, a light rain that continued throughout the day. I gathered palm fronds and built a lean-to against the tree. Not solid enough to keep the rain out, but enough to break its fall.

On the fourth day, while I was preparing my evening meal—boiled freshwater shrimp and papaya—a horse wandered into my clearing. Dog ran to the horse and walked around him sniffing. The horse ignored Dog. Dog ran to me to complain. Then, we heard the horse's owner call to him.

A boy walked into the clearing dragging a huge palm frond behind him. The boy was about eighteen years of age. He was nude. Two more young men followed him. They each wore a loincloth. "Hi," they said, one after the other.

I tried to look at them and not to look at them. They eyed my shrimp. "We eat only vegetables," one said, "Papaya, we eat only papaya. Ten or twelve a day." His belly was huge, distended. It hung over his loincloth. All three had huge, distended bellies. "Sometimes, we eat cocoanut," he said wistfully.

I gave them one of my cocoanuts.

"I've been here almost one year," said the talkative one. "They've been here almost two. We're hiding from the draft." He paused, lifted his loincloth, and urinated against the tree.

"I sleep in my poncho," I said. A long and vacant pause followed this pronouncement. "You should eat shrimp," I continued, "high protein." Again, they made no reply. I was conscious I hadn't eaten my evening meal and that soon it would be dark.

Then they were gone. Lightning streaked across the sky followed by the distance sound of thunder. Night came. I slept. An hour or so later, the rain, no more than a light drizzle at first, forced its way beneath my poncho and began to pelt my forehead. I could hear the water dropping through the branches, a "swish, gurgle, gurgle" from a nearby stream. Reaching out a hand for support, I felt it plunge beneath the rising water.

All at once, I longed for the comfort of a parked car, the glimmer of a light. The wind blew the rain through an opening in the roof. My hut collapsed; the sodden branches fell across me. Soon I was sleeping in the stream.

Absolutely black. Not a glow, not a glimmer, like the inside of a cave where bats go to hide during the day. I couldn't see the trail or even guess where it began. And I was lying in the water! I had to escape and had no way of escaping.

I spent the night standing, sleeping against the tree, and, of course, feeling generally sorry for myself. In the morning Dog was gone. The trail, too, had vanished. I was ready to go home and set out wading along the streambed. Where I could, I climbed the hillside to keep out of the water. Only after it was too late did I realize my mistake. I was on the wrong side of the valley.

Far off, an intermittent rumble could be heard, the sound of the waves striking the rock-strewn beach. Behind was the stream. Ahead, huge boulders barred my path to the beach. Tossed carelessly aside by an ancient volcano, each rock was a separate journey for me. Up, find a foothold, down. Never straight ahead.

The rocks grew smaller as I drew farther from the valley, and closer to the ocean. I could step with care from one to another. The shore wind grew in intensity as I walked, whipping the poncho over my head like an inside-out umbrella, forcing me to walk doubled over.

I came to where I could see the ocean. No beach here, no clean white sand. Waves fell directly on the stones, hissing as they sought to escape back to sea. Gray-green breakers rose a hundred yards or more from shore, built, crested, and smashed against the rocks.

Turning my back on the shore to confront the river, I saw that the main stream, forty yards wide and swollen by the rains, had drawn almost level with its banks. If I slipped while crossing, I would be swept out into the surf where the dull thud of the cleansing breakers repeatedly pounded the rocks. Afraid, I turned and walked back into the valley where I'd spent the night, where the stream was narrower and the waters calmer.

I walked until I could no longer see the sea, to where the sound of water dripping through the trees could compete with the hissing of the waves. The current was strong here, too, but I was just able to keep my balance. The water rose from my waist to my chest. It covered the shoes that I had slung around my neck. I stood on tiptoe for a moment fighting against the current. Then I had crossed the halfway point and the water began to go down again. On the far shore, I found Dog.

The climb out of the Valley was fatiguing, almost monotonous. Dog barked at my heels for most of the climb, barring her teeth. Near the top, I thought mainly about my hunger.

More walking and a couple of lucky rides. I retrieved my suit—it hadn't been cleaned or pressed and no one answered my knock—and headed for tourist land. My plan was to sleep in a hotel lobby, but the wrinkles in my suit gave me away. Within minutes, the hotel detectives rousted me.

"On your feet."

"I'm waiting for the airport limousine."

"Wait outside."

I moved a dozen times that night. During the day, I got by on the beach, sleeping, gazing at an ocean of browning flesh, winking at the broads, waiting to be discovered.

I wanted to be part of something. And, finally, Hawaii welcomed me. The banners were all over the Hotel district: "Welcome American Society of Systems Programmers and Computer Personnel." ASSPCP, that was me! A computer person for over four years, and an ASSPCP member. (At least, I had been when Missiles and Space was paying my way.)

"Hi, Jim. Jim?" a voice called out behind me.

Someone was calling my name.

It had started! I was just inside the door of the conference and I was practically back at work again!

I turned and the face and voice came together in my mind. "Hi Al, long time. . . ," I began.

"Jimbo. Good to see you. Kubreck spring for your trip to Hawaii? I should have joined you people. I'm a Programmer IV now though."

(Kubreck? Spring for a trip? Oh, yeah. Kubreck had all this talk about starting a consulting firm. I was going to be a vice-president. I'd even tried to recruit Al back then. But Al had stayed with Missiles and Space wanting the security. Smart move. Hey, maybe Al would recruit me! Maybe someone would.)

"Hi, Jim."

Someone else was saying hello to me. I knew the face, I couldn't remember the name. I answered "Hi," but the face didn't stop to chat. I knew the name that went with this next face: Dr. Barnes, my old section chief at M&S. He'd said he'd hire me back as soon as the group had an opening. "Hi, Doc."

Not even a "Hi" out of him in return, just a nod as he walked by.

"Don't worry about Dr. Barnes," Al said, "he's got a lot on his mind. You'll be seeing him at the banquet. All the gang will be getting together afterwards. You, too. Hey. Where you staying?"

"I'm... not registered yet."

"You gotta get registered." Al said.

We were in the registration line. The girl said, "Name?"

"Smith. James S. Smith."

She typed two lines and handed me a plastic badge that read, "Aloha, Hawaii welcomes you, ASSPCP 13th Annual, James S. Smith," along with a program guide and a map of Honolulu.

"Pre-registered?" the girl asked.

"Uh... Yeah."

"Can't find your name." The girl smiled. "This whole thing is so screwed up anyway. Doesn't matter. Dammed computers. Find your hotel OK?"

"They, uh, don't seem to have a record of my reservation."

"Hey Jimbo," Al put in, "I thought you were staying here."

"Shut up, Al," I prayed, hoping the sweat didn't show on my forehead, "Shut up."

The girl didn't seem to have heard him. Thank God. She was gorgeous, lovely, dark, Hawaiian, not Italian. She caught me looking. "Take this voucher over to the registration desk," she said. "You can straighten the whole thing out with InterCosmopolitan when you get back to Los Angeles."

I choked. "InterCosmo is handling the convention!"

"That's my employer. We handle conventions, tours and travel reservations. Do I look like a computer person?

"Have a nice time in Hawaii, Mr. Smith." A smile and she went on to the next registrant, "Name?"

As in a dream, I walked across the lobby, presented the voucher the girl had given me, signed the hotel register, and, fending off the tip-hungry bellmen, went to my room. I sat on the edge of the bed for a long time, staring at the view that $185 a day bought in Waikiki—the view, the color TV, and a set of luggage marked H. Krumball.

H (for Henry) was my size. H himself didn't show up for two more days. (Where had he been?) When he did, he accepted my apologies with an alcoholic's good grace and took back all his suits. For those two, three days I had a ball—banquets, luncheons, and long rap sessions at the pool. Girls in and out of every room. Women I had known before, women whose names I didn't catch. Guys who bought me drinks, guys who talked around the possibility—just the possibility—of a job back in L.A.

So I finally got back on the tour. And guess who else was there? Miss Mouse and her pudgy, dark friend. They weren't schoolteachers after all, but programmers like me! I gave them a big hello—like I would old friends from school, and avoided them whenever I could. It wasn't always easy. They had the same book of tickets I did, the little book InterCosmopolitan had left for Henry and me. It contained tickets for banquets (I left after the meal, before the opening speeches), a lunch with fashion show for the ladies (I stayed for the ladies), even a guided tour of Diamond Head.

Mousy Brown sat next to the strapping beach boy who drove the bus. I sat in the back with Dolly Ginsburg, (born Smith). Dolly just had to have the greatest pair of nose cones in the missiles and space business. She was also the life of every party until Al Ginsburg grounded her. (In private and afterwards, Dolly could be a bore. "I love Al. I should have stayed with Tom. Tom's no good. Al is so good to me. I don't know what to do..." and so on in a heavy nasal accent.) In public, with a little bit of booze inside here, Dolly was fun, fun, fun.

She had all of us in the back of the bus in stitches. I don't know whether those people knew one another when they got on the bus, but they sure knew one another when they got off. Everyone was getting up and changing seats and yelling back and forth and singing. You could hardly hear the PA system with its "Kamenhahemaha Day celebrates the coronation . . ." But the tour guide turned out to be a tremendous sport, and he led us all into Diamond Head singing at the top of our lungs.

So, it's all a memory. A nice memory, like that night in the Green Lobster, with no need to do anything but be. We're at Diamond Head, a bunch of crazies running around the parking lot. Giggling, too drunk to sing, passing a hurricane glass filled with rum. Then we're back at the hotel in Waikiki and they're taking down the exhibits.

The registration tables have been dismantled, the welcome signs replaced by something in Japanese. People are talking about the planes they're going to catch, shouting "Good-bye, see you in Boston." A few people are coming up to me, the ones I'd sort of thought I'd remembered, saying, "Hi, I thought it was you," and then they are gone too.

"See you in Boston." Even Henry showed up in time to pick up his bags and take back his suits again. (Where were you Henry? Where are you now?)

Two p.m.: check out time. I hung around in the lobby until six when the hotel detectives started to give me the eye. No way to blend, no one I could blend with. Unless... Across the lobby are my old friends, mousy brown and pudgy black. Pudgy has spent the intervening week growing a three-inch hair on her chin. She is still the cuter of the two. Mousy brown has a face like an axe head, pure New England, and a spare little body that says I want to be loved, lend me the equipment.

Mousy drags her friend forward, gives me the arm too, clinging. Black hair is the one that speaks, crooning the lyrics from a new reggae tune:

"In the Aquarian age, we understand,
Sometime, the woman, she ask the man."

We go to their room. They order me dinner. We spend the rest of the evening fucking. I fuck them on every piece of furniture in the room, on the rug, on the floor, in the bathtub. They know how to use their hands to arouse real passion. And they come conveniently often. I release one, top the other, keep moving. Pause, thrust, suck, keep stiff.

They screamed the whole time, pleasure mostly. They begged me to stop and they begged me to keep doing it. Not endearments, these were orders. I slept when they slept. When they woke I was made to be ready for them.

The idea came to me in the night, just the core of an idea, not the whole thing, that maybe this was the way it was supposed to be for me. The three of us together back in L.A. sharing an apartment. All of us working, with me taking turns to please them.

In the morning, after they had packed, the brown-haired one handed me two fifty-dollar bills without looking up at me, and I knew it wasn't going to be like that.

Part III: Unusual Bedfellows

The Silkie

I like the beach in the evening. The tourists have all gone home or are back in their motels. The beach becomes a special place just for those of us who live nearby.

My dad used to say the only reason he moved here with the rents so expensive is so we could spend at least one hour each day walking on the sand. My dad would come out of his den after dinner, usually while one or the other of us kids was still washing the dishes and say, "all right mother, let's all go to the beach." My father talked that way, using old-fashioned expressions.

My mom always was quick to answer for us, "The dishes aren't done yet, are they Diana?," but before I could start in dad would reply "Oh, leave them," and then we'd all walk or bike down to the beach together.

Sometimes there would be seals, hundreds of them in the water, and sometimes a line of dolphins just beyond where the waves were breaking. The dolphins hadn't been there during the day. It was as if the dolphins and the seal men had just been waiting for the tourists to go home, too.

And, maybe, as it got darker, it would just be me and my dad walking together along the shore above the wave line, while my sisters stayed with mom and built a fire or something.

My dad talked to me then in a way he never talked with me when we were at home. He told me about his life and all he'd thought of being. He told me about the time before he met mom, when he'd been a sailor in the war. He told me about some of the strange things he'd seen or had heard the other sailors talk about.

"There are people out there," he'd say, and he'd point beyond the line of breakers. "They look just like we do or almost, only they live under the sea. They are part man and part seal, and they herd the big fish for food, the way we herd cattle."

"Dad, you're being silly," I'd reply, scornfully. "I'm too big for stories like that." The strangest smile would come over his face. He'd look beyond me over my shoulder out to the water and say, "Look, Di, there's one of them, a silkie, now." And though I was too big to believe foolish stories and old enough to know there is no such thing as a silkie, I'd always look.

When it was very dark, and you couldn't see anything but the glow of the city and the lights of our campfire, we'd walk back and join the others. We'd have s'mores heated over the fire. We'd talk about what we'd done during the day. And, then, we'd go back home together.

Not that I always was doing things with my family. I had a life of my own. At school and with my own friends. There was even a time after Dad left when I had nothing to do with my family, when I hated them. My crazy period I call it. When I hung out with Jose and Pete and the others. When all I did was hang out and I didn't go to school.

I began by ditching class. When the school called my mother in and told her, I said, "Well, if I have to go to Spanish—(I think this was the class I'd been cutting)—I won't go to school at all."

And I didn't. I spent all day at the pier hanging out and sometimes I'd be there in the evening too, though it was different by the pier after it was dark.

The sky would go from bright blue to gray, the streetlights would come on, and all of a sudden there would be a vast dark hole where the sea had been. The crazies would show up then, fresh from tapping the source. They'd look you up and down as if you were a piece of meat or, if you were skinny like me, they'd try to borrow money or get you to do errands.

Once, this Hispanic dude, elegant in a white linen suit, parked his big white Cadillac next to where I was standing. He got out, not speaking, leaned against his car and looked out the length of the pier toward the invisible ocean. I wondered what he was thinking. There are street lamps on the pier, maybe every two or three hundred feet, but there are long dark stretches between and no one goes out there after dark.

Then he was standing next to me. "Kid," he said, "you take this ten bucks; you watch my car." I nodded my head, and he walked out on the pier.

He never came back. After awhile, when two of my friends drove by wanting to know what was happening, I let them drive me home.

I started going to the alternative school after that and soon I was back in the regular high school. The kids looked at me funny after I came back and I told mom I'd like to go to a different school, but she said, "No, we can't afford to move." So I did the best I could and tried to avoid the looks.

I tried to avoid the beach too, especially after dark. Guys go there at night to drink wine and I'm not as skinny as I used to be. Still, when mom or one of my sisters gets on my nerves, the beach is the only place I can go to be alone.

Usually, I go with another girl, or I tell my mom I am going with one; she doesn't think it is safe for me to go out on my own after dark. "Stay with your family," she says.

I take my bike, lock it under a street lamp, and then head into the darkness between the houses toward the beach.

I'm almost blind when I leave the streetlights. I walk slowly and carefully, and stop every few feet to listen. I don't want somebody jumping at me out of the darkness, not even a friend.

Sometimes, all I can hear is the wind. Other times, I might hear a voice, perhaps two voices, though I can't tell where the voices are coming from. It could be a couple sitting nearby in the darkness or a pair of joggers striding side by side farther away along the shore.

A jogger runs by me on the bike path and I move out of his way, startled. The wind changes direction. I can smell the sea and hear the waves. I stand for a long while, just breathing the air, becoming one with the sea and the sand.

A loud splash comes from directly in front of me. I can hear the sound of something large moving in the water, but I can't see what it is. For an instant, a cigarette glows in the darkness, or maybe it is a campfire rekindled by the wind. I strain my eyes and look out toward the water.

For a moment all is still, and then—splash—a big fish—it's a dolphin, leaps almost straight up, a saddle fitted just behind his dorsal fin.

If the man had said anything to me then, even, "will you look at that!" which is what I said when I saw the big fish—mammal—jump, I'd have moved away from him or left the beach entirely.

But he only smiled, a big warm smile, somewhere between a grin and a chuckle, like the smile my dad used to have when we were friends. I couldn't help smile back.

"Hi. I'm Daryl."

"I'm Di, Diana."

Daryl had been standing quietly only a few feet away. After we saw the dolphin, it seemed natural that Daryl and I would stand together and talk, first about the big fish—mammal, we'd seen, and then about the smell of the sea, and the sounds, and how in the evening the beach is a world of its own where you needn't feel rushed or afraid.

Daryl is very handsome. My dad only has a single hair on his chest and it takes him forever to grow a beard. Daryl always has the shadow of a beard along his jaw line. A dark sprout of hair shows at his collar from the pelt beneath.

When we kissed, just once that evening, his mouth had the taste of the sea, slightly salty. He is very strong, but his touch is gentle and reassuring, and he walked me back until I was underneath the streetlights where I'd parked my bicycle.

I started going down to the beach regularly in the evening, not really to see if Daryl would be there waiting, but he always was.

Each time we met, we talked about everything in the world. About what we were going to do when we grew up and some of the exciting things—not many in my case—we'd already done. Daryl was going to be a kind of fish farmer, raise fish instead of animals and keep them in open pens at sea.

"And ride seahorses on the Oregon current," I joked.
"Dolphins," he replied seriously.

I was going to be a schoolteacher. I made this decision when I started back to school. A special kind of teacher that would try to understand what kids were going through at home and help them make their schoolwork meaningful.

Daryl and I weren't really alone on the beach; but when we talked, it was as if we sat alone inside a charmed circle. Once a big dog who'd gotten loose and was biting and snapping at everything in his way came dashing toward us. He stopped when he was only a few feet away and then ran howling. And once a homeless man, his hair wild and unkempt, circled us for almost ten minutes, muttering.

I love you Daryl, I said once, but I don't think he heard me.

I don't want you to think I spent all my free time at the beach with Daryl. I had school and homework and after-school activities. I had a regular boyfriend, too.

Jack was my boyfriend's name. He'd take me to the movies and to football games. He'd already asked me to the prom. Once he asked if I wanted to go for a walk on the beach. It surprised even me when I said, "No, I don't like the beach." My mother, who'd been sitting across the room pretending to read, gave me a look over the top of her glasses. Maybe I didn't like Jack as much as I thought I did. Maybe I didn't want to go steady with him.

The final evening on the beach, Daryl said to me, "let's go to where I live." In my crazy period, I might have replied, "sure let's go." But now I knew what I wanted to do or thought I did. I was going to go to college. I was going to study to be a schoolteacher.

"What would I do there?" I asked.

"You'd teach."

"I don't know enough," I said.

"Sure you do, Diana; you know an awful lot my people don't."

I was proud Daryl thought so much of me. But my mother is right: When you know what you can do, you can admit what you don't know and try to change. "I can't go with you yet, Daryl," I said.

"Will you walk me down to the water?" he asked.

So I walked him down to the ocean and watched as his feet turned into flippers, and he slipped, flipped into a larger wave and disappeared in the light's reflection.

I haven't seen Daryl since, not that I often have the time to come to the beach now that I've started college. If he does comes back, will I go with him?

Margo and the Flying Dutchman

Since almost the turn of the century, the Cooks Corners Tavern has been located at the bend in the highway where El Toro turns into Trabucco Canyon. Few homes were in the area when the bar opened, the hillsides wooded and untracted; still, the tavern was popular from the beginning with bikers and anyone else who liked to roam the backcountry listening to the throttle of their exhaust and marveling at the moon-like landscape. "Just want a beer," they'd say to their old ladies and power off into the hills, ending inevitably at Cooks Corners for a beer or three.

The bar was a rough place in the beginning, filled with guys that liked to talk dirty and throw slightly smaller guys through its windows just for fun. Today, it's a yuppie attraction with a slick polished hardwood dance floor and a band they actually advertise, but you can still see one or two of the old crowd loitering at the edges.

"You see the guy down at the end of the bar," the bartender says to Margo.

Margo looks over to where the bartender is pointing and sees a man in his thirties, fastidiously dressed, his hair as neatly trimmed as if it had been cut only the day before. An attorney or maybe a regional sales manager, she guesses. The man fiddles with a ring on his left hand and slides it into his jacket pocket. "Married," Margo declares. "Yup," says the bartender. He pours a fresh Campari, Margo's drink, and brings it down to her.

"You're getting better," he says, and gives her the full one hundred volts of his smile. They've been playing the game for almost twenty minutes now. Margo and the bartender. She'll point out a man and he, newly found big brother, will give her twenty or thirty reasons why she ought to stay clear of him. Or, he'll point out a guy. "That one's right for you," he'll say. And she'll explain why the man just isn't her type.

The game is a way to pass the time. She knows that once the music starts she'll probably dance with all of them including the rejects, but at least she'll have sense enough, she hopes, even after two or four drinks, not to go home with any of them.

The bartender is a little old to be the youngster he pretends to be—he's pushing forty, but Margo likes him. She enjoys the free and easy way he talks with her, though it is obvious, already, his sideline is being attractive and attentive to older women. She wishes her own son, three years out of the Marines and still trying to find himself, was more like this man.

The bartender has his own thoughts about Margo. Well into her forties, with a wonderfully trim figure, the speckled blond hair in its tight feathered bob says "grandma," but the direct blue-gray eyes and the two firm breasts playing peek-a-boo at the top of her bolero blouse say, "come play with me." A boob job, he wonders? Nah. She doesn't seem the type. Comes across straight and direct, even innocent. He feels a flicker of easily discarded compassion. She'll do, he decides. It's tough making love to all these women, he mutters under his breath as he fixes three Vodka Collins and a white wine to hand to the waitress, but somebody's got to do it.

Eighteen years he has worked at Cooks Corners, ever since he dropped out of college. He flexes his shoulders thinking how it was in the old days: He and Jeb the other bouncer coming out together from behind the bar, the lead weights loose in the palms of their hands. He can still feel the jolt as the weights crack against someone's jaw, hear the cry of the girls taken on the pool table in the back room. All gone now. And the dollar drafts have been replaced by Coronas with a twist of lime for $3.00 a bottle. $3.50 on Saturday night.

He remembers tearing up and down the surrounding hillsides on a borrowed cycle, just taking off in the middle of his shift, riding until it is morning or simply time for another beer.

You can't do that today. Not when half the hills are covered by tract homes, oops, luxury dwellings with four bedrooms, den, wall-to-wall carpeting, Jacuzzi. Wouldn't that be something? Take the old broad home and play with her for an hour or two in her Jacuzzi?

Left alone, Margo is growing bored. Would the dancing never start? The bartender seemed lost in his own thoughts. Well, she would just play the game on her own. Who has come into the bar in the last twenty minutes?

Two balding men in spectacles wearing suits and ties. Forget them. She's had a husband too many that could pass for either one.

An equally muscular buddy joined the aging biker with the sawed-off sport shirt and tattooed biceps. Cute, especially the new one, but like the bartender said, much too risky.

The kid with the black leather jacket and the fawn colored aviator's scarf sat quietly by himself only two seats away. Dressed like one of those old-time brown and white photographs, everything in sepia tones, he is trapped, forever young, his boyish smile coupled with a look of pain.

She remembers an evening at home when she was fourteen or fifteen when she'd found her father sitting alone in the front room which normally was strictly reserved for company. A glass of scotch sat next to him on the coffee table untouched. He was staring into space, his lips slowly moving though no sound emerged. She stood for a while watching him, not speaking, and only gradually become conscious of her thin, almost transparent nightdress. Embarrassed, still wondering about his feelings, she slipped away.

Her father's lips were thin, much like her own. The lips of the boy with the aviator's scarf are thick, sensuous. He has a dimple in his chin.

"I hate this place," he says.

"Places like this?" she offers, feeling for his meaning.

"Yeah. Places like this. You want a beer or a hamburger. You come inside. And all of a sudden, it's so complicated. All of it." He waves his hands at the intricate mating rituals, the false smiles, the glassy stares.

"When the dancing starts," Margo begins, trying to make him feel more cheerful. "It'll seem more normal."

"I don't dance," he says. "Not vertically, anyway." Margo is shocked. She was expecting anything but this senseless comment.

The boy stammers an apology:

"I'm sorry," he says. "I was out of line. I feel stupid and embarrassed cause I don't know how to dance and I say something stupid and even more embarrassing to cover up for it.

"Forgive me," he says.

His reply pleases her. “You didn’t have to apologize, but thank you anyway. Tell me about yourself.”

“I like to drive my cycle, to drive all night long, flying over the hills.” He pauses, and again looks away embarrassed as if he’s revealed much more of himself than he intended to. He steps down from the barstool. “I’ll be back,” he says and, unexpectedly, stumbles as he takes his first steps on the sawdust-strewn floor. Margo sees one of his legs is twisted and shorter than the other. “Don’t go,” she calls, then wonders why she is calling, why she is attracted to someone so different from herself.

She looks about her for her friend the bartender. Counsel me, she wills, but the bartender, deep in conversation with a hard-looking blond at the other end of the bar, does not look her way.

Thinking about the young man in the leather jacket, she is very conscious of the difference in their ages. “But it’s not your age that’s important,” she admonishes herself, something she’s learned to do in the many therapy groups she’s attended since her divorce, “It’s how you feel about things and whether you and the other person share those feelings.”

The young man returns. God, he is handsome. A flush takes over her entire body and she turns away, conscious the glow can be seen traveling up her face and neck. She looks down at her glass, then up just in time to catch the bartender’s eye.

She clutches at her one remaining advantage. “Tell me who he is,” she whispers to the bartender, gesturing toward the young man in the aviator jacket.

The bartender takes a quick look and seems to recognize the man, but when he looks back at Margo, he acts confused and unsure of himself. Could he be frightened? The bartender's lips work for a few moments with no sound coming out. "I think he's been in before," the bartender says finally, bending down so his mouth is only a few inches from Margo's ear, "A long time ago," he whispers, "before I started working here even. But I don't know who he is."

You're lying, Margo thinks; she is sure of it. As soon as the bartender steps away, she asks the young man the same question: does he know the bartender?

"Yeah. He used to be one of the guys I rode with."

I thought so, Margo says to herself. But then why didn't the bartender tell me that to begin with? Something is wrong and she ought to get up and walk away. But the band is warming up now and in a few minutes the dancing will begin. She turns to the young man to ask if he would like to dance and then remembers his leg. Embarrassed and confused, she remains on her stool not speaking.

The bartender has poured her another Campari; the young man has paid for it.

"Do you want to go for a ride?" he asks, breaking the silence.

"A ride?" she repeats, stalling for time. A ride on his motorcycle? She hasn't been on the back of a cycle for years. This is crazy. She doesn't even know him. The young man stands up, pushing down hard with one hand on the bar stool to take the weight off his injured leg. Is he going without her?

"Yes," she says, "I'll go for a drive with you."

The motorcycle is much larger than she expected. How do you get aboard it, she wonders. He gets on easily enough, standing in the stirrups to kick the cycle's engine alive.

She looks at the vehicle warily, still looking for a way to step up onto the seat. There is a great deal she wants to ask the young man before they leave, but his back is to her, and the sound of the cycle is already loud in her ears.

"Just jump on," he says, glancing back briefly over his shoulder. He is wearing his aviator goggles now and his eyes are as invisible as a motorcycle policeman's.

She slips one leg half-on, half-over the seat, exposing an awkward length of thigh. She is still looking for something to hold on to, when the motorcycle jerks forward leaving her no choice but to throw her arms around him for support.

He smells a little like a sweaty horse, like dusty highways, a little of tobacco and beer.

The motorcycle comes to an abrupt halt at a traffic light and she is thrust against him, her thighs sliding forward along the seat, her breasts pushing against his back. A warm glow suffuses her body as she feels the pressure of his back against her sensitive nipples and thighs. She thinks suddenly of his full-lipped mouth. Then, they are flying along the road.

Where are we going, she wonders. "Where are we going?" she asks, and to her own amazement adds, "My place is just up the hill."

Why did she say that? She doesn't want him coming back to her place, not yet and perhaps not ever.

But her ghost rider does not reply. They fly over the hills, deep into the inner canyons, the wind streaming by her face, her body pressed against his, the roar of the motorcycle's engine loud in her ears.

For a short while, she tries to keep track of where they are going, but it is too difficult to see, and too often her thoughts shift to the soft skin at the back of his neck, to what it would be like to feel his chest and thighs unclothed against hers.

She looses track of time as well. Is the dance lesson over now? Will I be late for the eleven o'clock news?

Where are they going? Trabucco Canyon, Silvarado, Mossback Hill, she no longer even recognizes the names.

Talk to me, she wills, but her ghost rider does not speak.

They round a curve. Hold on, she thinks, and grips him tighter.

The constant jostle of the moving vehicle, the seat tight beneath her thighs, the nearness of his body, break through her last defenses. An incandescence spreads through her entire body. My God, she thinks, I'm having an orgasm. And then she is having three, four orgasms in a row as the last of the twilight fades, the city lights recede in the distance, and an entire galaxy of stars spreads across the sky.

Rain

Rain was falling by the time Pinkie reached the campground, his newfound friend clinging to his arm, an intermittent rain that came and went erratically. Sometimes the rain consisted of large tear-shaped drops that splattered when they fell, and sometimes, a fine mist barely moistened the surface of his clothes.

Many of the men seemed to glory in the rain, not even bothering to put on their shirts, but Pinkie put on his baseball cap immediately, tilting the brim upwards. He did not like the way his head looked when his fine blond hair was plastered against his skull, pink, like a baby's ass.

Rain had been falling on and off at the beach for several days now. Nothing really got soaked through, but nothing got quite dry either. When someone offered him a lift north, Pinkie leaped at the opportunity. Surely, it would be warm and dry farther north. But the storm clouds that hung off the California coast extended from the Mexican border to San Francisco.

The changes confused him. The familiar flat lands covered with oil-derricks gave way to crowded city streets, burnt-brown hills, and then the coast again, a narrow strip of highway nestled against the cliffs. When they stopped for gas, Pinkie asked to be left behind.

For some moments, he remained by the side of the highway, trying to accept his new environment, staring vacantly at the pavement. A single large raindrop fell on his nose. Another, and another. Slowly, he began to walk south, parallel to the ocean, at an angle to the direction in which he had come.

At a traffic light, Pinkie was joined by a second, equally bedraggled figure, perhaps five or six years younger. The man talked to himself as he walked, "Don't pay attention. Details aren't important. I told Bentley."

At first, Pinkie thought the man's presence just coincidence. But he stayed too close to Pinkie, dashed forward whenever Pinkie's steady pace left him behind, and stood waiting for Pinkie to catch up when, seemingly, some inner agitation had driven him on ahead. He was like a stray dog that will sometimes take up with a person on the highway, darting forward, dropping back, ending inevitably by his new master's heels as if he always has and always will belong there.

"Don't pay attention. No one listens to Peter," the man said.

When Pinkie stopped to look at the ocean, Peter began to urinate, seemingly oblivious to the cars and pedestrians passing only a few feet away. Pinkie was indignant. Didn't the man realize where they were? Thank God, I'm not like him. Most of the time, he corrected, momentarily ashamed.

The rain continued to fall, though the sun still shone brightly on the sea to their right. To their left, the green hills disappeared in the mist. A moment more and there was only the sea and the mist; even the highway, a few feet to their left, was all but invisible.

Pinkie's new companion left the pavement and skipped, slid down the embankment. Pinkie hesitated; then he, too, clambered downwards following the coastline as it curved out and away from the highway. In less than a minute, the last of the coast road's sights and smells were gone.

A trailer park loomed out of the mist ahead of them. A few middle-aged couples still sat outside beneath their awnings, tending their barbecues or playing cards, seemingly unconcerned by the intermittent rain. Other older occupants were mere shadows behind their blinds. "What will become of me when I am old?" wondered Pinkie, his stomach contacting in a momentary wave of fear, "I haven't got a home."

Peter seemed to be regaining his confidence now they were well away from civilization. "Good food. Good company," he stammered, trying to share his joy, and skipped along the path.

In a few minutes, they were perched on a low embankment overlooking a dry creek. Only a few steps more and they had reached a shantytown of tents and lean-to's set along a dry riverbed. The highway could be seen overhead, suspended on trestles where it crossed the canyon from north to south. Though tiny windup cars crossed back and forth high above them, the only sound was of the nearby surf.

Some of the homeless had tents, some lean-to's built of driftwood and logs washed down from the canyon above, and some, like Pinkie's new friend, had just tossed their bedrolls down on the gravel. Entire families strolled up and down and played together. Almost everyone smiled, and most said "Hi" to Pinkie. A father rolled a ball to his child; "Buenos, Maria," the mother cried out, laughing, as the child took it in her grasp.

Pinkie's face spread in a wide grin as the tension fled his shoulders. He felt relaxed, comfortable, and, for once, unafraid.

Peter led them toward a common cooking fire. Though the two men had nothing of their own to contribute, their plates were soon heaped with supper—a mixture of squirrel meat and hamburger with carrots and potatoes in a pan. While Pinkie ate, he studied the girl who sat across the fire from him. In her late twenties, her arms were firm and tanned, the muscles taut and rippling beneath the skin; she seemed very strong and assured, almost fierce in her movements.

She doesn't really belong here, he thought; she's like me and just has no other place to go.

"D'ya think she noticed me?" he said to Peter. Plate in hand, Pinkie moved to the other side of the fire, a step or two at a time, until he stood next to the girl. She turned and gave him a long penetrating stare.
A long jagged scar ran from just under her right ear to almost the bridge of her nose. A knife wound. She's not like me, he thought, repelled, but before he could break contact, the girl reached out her hand. "What's your name?" she asked, her accent calling up visions of Appalachia. "Pinkie," he said. "Noreen," and she pumped his hand up and down in a firm grasp.

It began to rain in earnest then; Pinkie even thought he could hear thunder up in the canyons. What had been an inconvenience earlier in the day when the sun slipped in and out of the clouds, turned deadly as the community scattered to seek for shelter before the onset of darkness. I don't have any spare clothes, Pinkie thought; all my spares are hidden back at the other beach. I don't have any poncho either, what am I going to do?

"You can get under my rain blanket with me," the girl with the scar called to him. She stood in the same place she had been standing only a few minutes before, seemingly oblivious to the drops that pelted her face and forehead. "C'mon," she hollered, "You can't just stand there like a stick."

She must think I'm a dummy, Pinkie said to himself. She doesn't know I can think good, better than most people.

The girl literally dragged Pinkie across the riverbed to where her possessions were hidden beneath a tree, wrapped in a plastic tarpaulin. She pulled an edge of the tarpaulin free and sat down on a log next to the embers of a still smoldering campfire. Spreading the tarp over her head and shoulders, she indicated a spot next to her on the log. When Pinkie sat down, she spread the cover over both their shoulders. "Thanks," he said stiffly.

A few minutes later, Peter came shuffling by in the darkness. He looked as if he would like to sit down between Pinkie and the girl, and, when neither made room for him, as if he wanted to sit on the girl's other side. Finally, Peter contented himself with a space on the ground next to Pinkie on the side furthest from Noreen, not quite in and not quite out of the tarpaulin.

Pinkie was tired, but sleep, the deep recuperating rest he needed, stayed just out of reach. He relived the events of the day—the fishermen who had woken him early that morning, the series of rides that had led him up the coast, the long walk along the highway, his new friend Peter snuffling at his heels, the camp, Noreen's strong hand in his. . . .

Once or twice he woke and was conscious of the girl next to him and the steady sound of the still falling rain. He could hear the surf then, its angry pounding less than a quarter mile away at the mouth of the dry creek bed. He slept again listening to the rain.

Toward morning he was conscious of a rising in his groin; Noreen's hand was in his lap, an accident? He let his hand rest on her knee, then slid it down the inside of her thigh and touched her between her legs. She moaned and held his wrist in place. She pressed her upper body against his; her lips were on his lips; her scar was pressed against his cheek.

"God damn, shit," came Peter's voice from out of the darkness. What was he complaining about? The rain? The cold? Some black memory of his own? Almost but not quite dawn, the continuing darkness must be endured.

"Got to take a piss," Peter hollered. Be polite, Pinkie thought, there are women here. Noreen's hand massaged his neck; her mouth sucked greedily at his own. Will she let me touch her breast?

"God damn." Peter again. Pinkie and Noreen heard the sounds of a splash, then a series of splashing sounds. "Water," Peter hollered. All around them newly awakened men and women were hollering, "Water! The river!"

"I can feel it," Noreen said. Indeed, Pinkie could feel it; the cold water was up to and over his boots.

"Got to get the rest of my stuff," Noreen said. "No," Pinkie warned her, "We've got to get to high ground." He headed instinctively toward the rise, in the opposite direction to that Peter had taken. Peter, where was Peter?

"Maria," he heard a woman call frantically. A torrent of cries followed in both English and Spanish, loud splashing sounds, and then a roar as if the surf were only inches instead of a half mile away.

"Noreen," he called, feeling the water tug at his legs. Pinkie fought the current the last few steps up the short rise that formed the south bank of the dry creek; then, he was at the top: how could the water still be pulling at his legs? He ran blindly, desperately, heading for the hillside, pursued by the tireless roar of the rapidly moving flood.

A chorus of voices cried out frantically behind him. "Noreen," Pinkie whimpered. Darkness everywhere, the familiar warm glow of the city swallowed by the storm clouds, and still no signs of the coming dawn.

Slowly, all too slowly, the sky turned from black to gray. Dawn—dark and gloomy, but dawn nonetheless. Pinkie stood with the hill at his back, perhaps two hundred yards farther south and twenty or thirty feet above where he had spent the night. The wide raging river of the early morning had subsided, but the now-empty riverbed bore no signs of those who had slept there the night before. Muskrats and waterfowl had reclaimed the mud flats; a narrow stream flowed down the center of the valley where the homeless had once camped.

I got to go, thought Pinkie. He tried walking farther up the hill, but slipped downwards on the slippery surface. He fell half a dozen times before he turned to follow along the edge of the new stream the river had carved to the shore.

A helicopter went by overhead; first, Pinkie heard the whirring sound and then, as if by accident, he saw the helicopter's outline revealed in the mist. A man with a video camera leaned out taking pictures of the trailer park. "But what about us?" Pinkie thought, "What about us?"

Another twenty minutes and he reached the coast highway. A wall of mud and fallen rock had blocked the road to the north. A line of cars waited patiently, though it was not clear when the highway would reopen. "When the rain stops," Pinkie heard someone say, but the rain showed no signs of stopping.

Several of the drivers had stepped out of their cars, and were standing together, talking in low tones. "On TV," someone said and pointed to the clouds overhead where the still barely visible helicopters buzzed in and out.

A battered black Corvette left the line in reverse, did a quick U over the highway median, and settled with a thump facing south. The car raced forward and was almost out of sight when it reversed a second time and pulled alongside Pinkie. The young driver stuck his head out the Corvette's window and asked, "You want a lift old-timer?"

"Sure," Pinkie said, though he didn't much like being called old-timer. "Thank you," he added. In a moment, they were racing southward toward more familiar beaches.

Part IV: Breaking Up Is Very Hard to Do

Bloody Marys

(Adapted from the novel *San Onofre*)

“Well, here you are,” she said, opening the front door of her apartment and rousing him from his daydream. She placed her small hand inside his large one and led him into the front room. “I've fixed us some drinks.” She handed him a tall glass filled with a red liquid. “Here. Drink it.”

“What?” he said, flinching momentarily.

“Drink it.”

He hesitated. “I, I, I mean what is it?”

“I, I, I,” she repeated, “What do you need to know for? I said, ‘drink it.’” She thrust the glass at him a second time. “Do you think I'm trying to poison you?”

He shook his head.

“Drink it.”

For some reason, he found it difficult to look at her. The plunging neckline of her housecoat revealed her nipples jutting out at him like two large eyes. He wanted very much to have sex with her—now—without any preliminaries.

The tall glass of liquid in her hand looked like tomato juice. He took a sip and choked. “That's not tomato juice.”

“You are such a baby. Now take another sip, a bigger one this time.”

He reached for the glass, but she would not let go of it, forcing him to stand on tiptoe while he drank. He took a quick sip, trying to pull away from her hand, but she kept the glass tilted until he'd drunk almost half of it. She released it only when he began to make choking sounds.

"You are a virgin. Don't you ever drink alcohol?"

"I drink beer." A hurt, almost puzzled expression crossed his face.

"I bet you do, as much as a bottle at a time. Here, eat this stalk of celery, maybe it will help."

She poured herself a second glass from the pitcher and took a sip from it, watching until he'd finished the glass she'd given him.

"Well?"

He felt very warm and slightly dizzy. "I, uh, thought we might go for a bike ride this evening, to get some exercise."

"A bike ride?" she echoed, a teasing lilt in her voice.

"To get some exercise."

"I'll give you all the exercise you need." She put her arm under his and grasped his fingers, locking his arm against her as she did so. They walked into her bedroom.

After they'd had sex—she'd made him come twice before conceding her own satisfaction—she sat propped up on the pillows smoking a cigarette, while he lay flat on the bed beside her. "You're really going to have to get a room," she said.

He sat up startled.

“And you’re going to have to start taking showers. You smell awful.”

“But I just got home. I didn’t have time to. You wouldn’t let me. What do you mean, I’ll have to get a room?”

“Well you can’t stay here all the time.” She blew a lazy puff of smoke toward the ceiling. “I may have to have someone come and stay with me. Besides, I need my privacy.”

“Who?”

“Who what?”

Angrily he grasped her shoulders, “Who is coming to stay with you?”

She pushed his arms away. “Well, my daughter for one, and her husband, and their triplets. I am a grandmother, you know.”

“No I didn’t know. When are they coming?”

“Who?”

“Your daughter, her husband.” He couldn’t bring himself to mention the triplets, to think of her as a grandmother.

“Not for awhile, but you’ve got to get yourself moved out of here. It’s just too messy.”

“But. Does this mean? Will we?”

“Of course, we will. I just don’t want the mess. Look, I’m going to give you a drawer. The things you absolutely need, fresh underwear and a clean shirt for when you do stay overnight, you put in the drawer. Everything else just has to go. I've already started a pile for you."

"Where will I go?"

"You'll get a room."

"There are no rooms."

"Oh, don't be ridiculous. There are plenty of rooms."

"There are no rooms around here, I've looked. And the motels are worse."

"Yes," she said, remembering the one night they'd spent together in a local motel. She'd insisted he come to her house after that. "Well you'll just have to keep looking."

He made a gasping sound.

"Oh for God's sake. I'll make the call for you." She stubbed out her cigarette, threw back the covers revealing her long shapely legs, and stalked into the living room. He came after her, slipping on his pants as he went.

"Mildred? Yes I am fine. Do you have room for another young man? I recommend him. Highly. Well, he was a student. At Berkeley. I'm sure he'll fit in with those other brains of yours.

"Well," she said, as she hung up the receiver, "I've found you a room. Aren't you proud of me?"

"Where is it?"

"Next to the University."

"The University! That's twenty miles from here."

She looked at him closely as if seeing him for the very first time. It seemed plain to him that she did not like what she saw. "Well, that's a lot closer than going in all the way to Los Angeles to be with your girlfriend."

"My girlfriend," he echoed, gradually turning beet red. How did she know about Lenore?

"Your girlfriend. When a man hasn't had a woman in a while, he's not able to control himself, and when he finally gets the opportunity, the little dear, he comes all in a burst. You go away for a night, you come back a better lover than ever. Ergo, you have a woman and you've slept with her."

"Do you want me to go?" he said quietly, very quietly, as if afraid she would hear and order him to go.

"Not yet," she said and poured the remains of the pitcher of Bloody Marys into her glass, "I think we may as well have some more bicycle riding as you call it."

The Divorce

When Pinkie wakes, he is lying on the beach only a few yards from the water. Somehow, during the night, he had left his pallet by the food stall and wandered across the sand. His vision is blurred; he has a sense of figures just outside his line of view drifting to and fro like tropical fish. When his eyes clear, the few early-morning swimmers have moved past him down to the water and are already knee deep in the surf.

All of a sudden, his mind moves him back thirty years to when he is living near Lloyd Shoals with his uncle. During the summer, Pinkie bikes down to the lake every day with his cousins and they go swimming or just lie around on the grass near the boat access and talk.

His cousins have lots of friends, girls as well as boys. They play games in the water, tag and keep-away. Pinkie remembers hollering "Marco Polo" over and over one hot summer afternoon. There is a raft, too, he remembers, in the far corner of the lake, from which the older children take dive after dive.

As the surfers and other early-risers move around him keeping a careful distance, Pinkie thinks of the sudden hush whenever the Jukes came down to the lake. They are dirty, unkempt. Even at school, Steve Jukes often looks as if it were weeks since he last took a bath. And now, the Jukes are here, bathing in Pinkie's private swimming hole. Making it as dirty as they are.

Pinkie—he was called Ted then—is not surprised when Steve Jukes' mother takes out a bar of soap, begins to wash Steve's younger brother, Brian, then hollers at Steve to "come clean hisself up."

Ted, that is Pinkie, is glad when Steve's mother calls him back. Steve had been on his way out to the swim area, dog-paddling furiously, heading straight for Ted. I wouldn't have pushed him away like some of the other boys, but I'd have been embarrassed. We were all embarrassed to see the Jukes taking a bath in public like that.

One after another, the mothers gather their families' things and prepare to leave. But to go with them, Pinkie and his cousin will first have to swim through the narrow opening where the Jukes stand soaping themselves.

There is one other alternative—the raft. By the time Steve has finished washing and rinsing his hair, the older children have all swum out, too far from shore for Steve—a poor swimmer—to think of joining them. "Don't want Steve Juke's cooties," someone on the raft, Arvin, Barbara's younger brother says . . .

"How'd you like to have his cooties?" calls the taller of the two surfers, pointing at Pinkie's supine figure. He flicks the other, shorter boy with his towel. The two boys like the water, come down every morning before school, and are beginning, surreptitiously, to look at the bikini-clad girls who watch them. The second boy, an Asian, hollers back, jerking his thumb toward Pinkie, "Maybe we should throw him in the water, do him good."

I bathe every day, Pinkie thinks, but he doesn't argue with the boys. Slowly and with as much dignity as he can muster, he walks away down the beach. Later that morning, he notices the girl for the first time.

She is wearing a dark earth-colored skirt and a plain green tunic with short sleeves. Her arms are tanned and muscular, very attractive. The one discordant note is a pair of dark brown panty hose riddled with holes. She reminds Pinkie of someone. But who? when?

The night, less than a year ago, comes back to him: Her name is Noreen. He is seated beside her on the log, a plastic tarpaulin thrown across their shoulders. The rain is falling softly, steadily. He remembers the smell of Noreen's hair, the stronger smell of her desire. Before he can unbutton his clothing, they hear a splash, someone nearby cursing. "Pinkie, what's wrong?"

His legs are wet, that water is all around them. He stumbles; the rain-swollen river catches at his pant legs. "Noreen" he calls, over and over, but the girl, too, has disappeared into the black night, the steadily falling rain.

One instant, Pinkie is back at that terrible time of panic, the next he is on the familiar beach standing in the warm sunlight with the now-open food stalls off in the distance. The girl is gone. "Couldn't have been her," Pinkie thinks. "Couldn't have been her," he says aloud.

But he sees her again that afternoon and a third time the following morning. It is Noreen, it has to be; somehow, she too escaped the flood.

Each time Pinkie sees Noreen, she is in the company of the same two men. The first is thin, silver-haired, non-descript, much like Pinkie himself. The other is short but muscular. A torn gray work shirt from which the sleeves have been removed reveals a pair of bulging biceps and thick, tattooed shoulders.

"He's been in the navy," thinks Pinkie.

"Prison more likely," says John the Barber, hovering by Pinkie's side, "Prison for sure."

"I know her," Pinkie says.

"You told me, seven times already."

Pinkie nods. "I know her," he repeats.

Noreen looks over to where Pinkie is standing, smiles and takes two quick steps in his direction. Her two male companions follow close behind.

"Hi," Noreen says as soon as she is within hailing distance.

Pinkie waves back shyly.

"I'm sorry, I've forgotten your name," she says.

"Pinkie."

"This is Dan." She points to the short man. Up close, he is even more menacing.

"You got any money?" Dan demands.

Pinkie begins stammering. He doesn't like it when he stammers; he is ashamed stammering like this.

"Dan," Noreen remonstrates, "Pinkie doesn't have any money; he's the same as you and me. And if he did have money, he'd share it with us. Wouldn't you?"

Pinkie fumbles in his pockets, looking for change; he would give all he had to Noreen if he could find some money, but, of course, he doesn't have any.

"We want to get divorced," Noreen says giggling, pointing to Dan. "Can you help us?"

"Can't stand the bitch," Dan calls out at the same time as he puts an arm around the girl. The other man, thin as the knife blade Pinkie can see hidden under his shirt, says nothing.

"You want to stay away from them," John the Barber whispers in Pinkie's ear. But Pinkie, hypnotized, cannot tear himself away from Noreen.

"I'll help you," he says.

"What do you know about getting a divorce?" Dan challenges. Everything Dan says is a challenge; he makes no attempt to hide the violence only inches from his surface.

"I know where the courthouse is," Pinkie says.

"You divorced?"

Pinkie nods his head.

"Guy's a loser," Dan says to his two companions, but Noreen, Pinkie is pleased to see, pays Dan no attention.

"You'll help us Pinkie?" asks Noreen.

Pinkie nods a second time.

"Let's go to the courthouse then," snarls Dan.

"Tell them 'later'" whispers John the Barber. But it is too late—the threesome is already walking toward the bus stop.

Somehow, thankfully, they have lost the other man, the one with the knife. Noreen whispers to Pinkie, "I like you, Pinkie, I always have, since that time, you know, when we were together."

Pinkie smiles, remembering, and then he recalls the rain again and the flood and wonders how Noreen can still be alive.

She explains as they cross the highway using her hands as much as her voice to tell the story. She ran as he did, though in a different direction, farther inland. As soon as it was light, she followed the crumbling path to higher ground and then back to the road. She met Dan two or three months ago. "He says we're married, but I don't think we are," she whispers to Pinkie. "This divorce will get rid of him."

"You got money for the bus?" Dan demands.

Pinkie shakes his head. He is afraid to speak when Dan is this close to him, afraid he will set Dan off. "We'll hitchhike then." Dan sticks out his thumb.

"What do we do now?" Pinkie asks when it is clear the cars will not stop.

"We let Noreen do the work," Dan snarls and makes a harsh gesture with his fingers.

A car stops almost the instant the two men step into the bushes, but Noreen makes no attempt to get in. "What the fuck," Dan says. The driver is leaning over the passenger seat gesticulating in Noreen's direction. They hear her swear violently and make an obscene gesture at the driver. "What the fuck," Dan says a second time, "Go find out what the fuck she thinks she's doing."

"Two seater," Noreen explains as they draw close to her, "Guy thought I was some kind of hooker. Said he liked dirt. I'm not dirty am I, Pinkie?"

Pinkie touches her wrist gently, reassuringly.

"He treats me like I am." She points an accusing finger at Dan.

"Shut your mouth, bitch. And get us a lift." Again the men hide themselves beside the road.

A second car stops, an older model Cadillac, but clean and shining as if it has just been washed. They can see Noreen talking with the driver. She gestures toward them.

"Now you go," Dan says to Pinkie, "don't fuck up."

Noreen waits until Pinkie reaches the car then slides into and across the front seat until she sits next to the driver, an elderly gray-haired man. She motions to Pinkie to sit down next to her. Pinkie isn't sure how or when it is accomplished, but Dan has slipped into the back seat behind them.

"Who is he?" asks the elderly man, jerking his finger toward Dan in the rear-view mirror. "Brother," Noreen replies laconically.

There is a long pause. Pinkie is counting the intersections they pass through—ten, twelve, fifteen, and then they are at the freeway. "Got a daughter just like you," the man says to Noreen, "Got three daughters; don't have any sons though."

"How far you goin' man?" Dan interrupts.

"I'm going to the mall, that's what I told the young lady."

“We’re going to the courthouse. Maybe you could drop us?”

“That’s a little out of my way.”

“Please,” Noreen says, “It would help us a lot.”

“Well. . .,” the man begins; you can tell he is more flattered than annoyed by the request; maybe Noreen does remind him of his daughter.

“Son of a bitch, make up your mind,” Dan says suddenly, unnecessarily from the back.

“I don’t think so,” the man says. At the next intersection, he pulls into the curb.

“You asshole,” Noreen says to Dan when they are out of the car. “Now we got to walk.”

“Shut up bitch. Talks too much,” Dan says to Pinkie. “Women talk too much, don’t you agree?” Pinkie shakes his head, looks down at his shoes embarrassed.

“Well fuck you both,” Dan says and begins to walk ahead of them. Pinkie smiles as Noreen takes his hand in hers. But in a few moments Dan is back, his presence intruding on their happiness.

“You know how to get the divorce do you?” he asks Pinkie, though he has already asked the same question, twice, on the beach.

“I know how to get the papers.”

"That's all we need," Dan says, "the papers. The bitch and I agree on everything. No kids. She can't have kids, you know that?"

For an instant, the brave smile vanishes from Noreen's face, an instant only, then, deformed, the smile comes out again. Pinkie wants to hit Dan, wants to hit him over and over, but he knows it is impossible. Shame takes the place of anger, almost bends him in two. Dan, content he has left nothing but ill feelings behind him, moves several paces in front again.

The Court House appears on the skyline ahead, one of a half dozen buildings situated in a two-block "Government Row."

"Where are we going?" demands Dan. Pinkie points in the direction of the Court House. "O.K." Dan says, and reorienting himself sets off again as if he were their leader rather than an unwelcome addition to the party.

Gradually, the three find themselves aligned with others heading in the same direction. At a traffic light, several attorneys in suits and ties discuss limited partnerships and a new, cleverer way the shorter of the group—he has jet black hair, his suit looks hand-tailored—has found to "package the deal." None of them pays the slightest attention to Pinkie and his friends.

Pinkie realizes he is no longer looking up and using the tall buildings as landmarks. He's simply following the men, trusting they will take him where he wants to go. The closer they get to the courthouse, the tighter Noreen holds his hand, and even Dan, still muttering audible blasphemies, stays close by.

When they cross at the final traffic light, the attorneys fall silent. Unexpectedly, the plaza before the courthouse is filled with the shopping carts of the homeless: Rows and rows of shopping carts, like rows of townhouses. Each cart holds one or more plastic garbage bags and is capped by a silver-gray blanket bearing a faint stenciled blue number.

Ragged, unkempt men and women sit nearby. Many are quite young, high school age, though there are no really young children. Blacks, Hispanics, Whites sit in separate areas; a few interracial couples huddle together along the boundaries.

The men and women are all strangers to Pinkie, but Noreen and Dan seem to know many of them. Dan, in particular, receives greetings on either side. Shy by nature, Pinkie distrusts the men who greet Dan so effusively. He has seen others like them on the beach, heavy drinkers who are quick to anger, to steal, to run away leaving others to take the responsibility.

When they reach the courthouse, Pinkie is surprised to find he's being sent in alone. He does not like leaving Noreen with Dan, and is unsure where in the immense multi-level building the Clerk's office is located. But he is afraid of Dan's anger if he appears hesitant. "You hurry back," Dan admonishes him as he leaves.

A half hour later, Pinkie returns empty handed. "It's six dollars for the forms," Pinkie says, "I don't have six dollars."

"Well," Noreen says, turning to Dan, "You said you'd pay for the divorce."

The small crowd of men standing beside Dan look interested. "I said I'd pay and I will pay," Dan says. He turns to Pinkie and steps forward and very close as if he were about to shake him. "You sure it's six dollars," he challenges as he reaches into his pocket.

"Y'yes," Pinkie stammers, "you can come with me, hear for yourself."

"Don' like courthouses. Already told you. You go get them papers. Oh, and Pinkie . . ."

Pinkie has already started toward the courthouse, the six crumpled bills in his hand, but stops and turns obediently.

"You can keep the change," Dan guffaws. The crowd of homeless men crow their appreciation. "Not very funny," Noreen says. "C'mmer bitch," Dan coos and grabs her to him.

An elegantly coiffured and perfumed woman, walking in intense conversation with another moneyed matron, glances at Dan indignant, but is forced to look away from his hardened stare.

"Why does Noreen let him?" Pinkie asks as he walks back inside the building. "Why does she stay with him?" She's afraid, he thinks, answering his own question, like I'm afraid.

A short strawberry-haired woman is standing on the courthouse steps in conversation with two other lawyers. "I know that man," she says when Pinkie walks by.

"Oh, made out a living will for him, did you?" The taller and better dressed of the two male lawyers chuckles at his own great sense of humor.

"This entire plaza is a living organ bank," says the second man and laughs also.

"Not funny," says the woman. "Besides, he's not from here. He lives on the beach, in my father's old neighborhood. I ran into him when I was closing up the house after Dad went to the hospital."

"What did you do with your father's old place?"

"I'm still thinking about selling it, but the market's off."

The two men cluck sympathetically. "I could use another rental." the shorter one says. "Near the beach is it?"

The woman makes a fluttering motion with her hand.

"Lower your price."

"I'm going to do just that."

"These are tough times . . ." begins the shorter of the two men, but he is interrupted again by the taller, "You could turn it into a shelter for the homeless."

"I don't think so," the woman says after a moment's pause. The man intended his comment as a joke, but sees, incredibly enough, that the woman took it seriously.

"They're probably just as comfortable here," says the shorter man with the slightly acrid after-shave, surveying the hundred or so shopping carts beneath him in the plaza, "like clings to like."

"What's it like," the woman wonders aloud, "being homeless?"

"Not pleasant," says the tall man, seemingly searching for a way to persuade the woman he can be serious, "Cold, hunger and not a hell of a lot of sex," he finishes with a guffaw.

This time when Pinkie returns he has the forms with him. Dan grabs for them immediately but Pinkie steps back out of his way. "The woman said they have to be typed."

"Typed? What the fuck for?" Dan demands.

"She said they had to be typed."

"Do I look like a fucking secretary? You type," Dan says to Noreen.

"I don't know how."

"I do," Pinkie says.

Dan looks scornful.

"Oh thanks, Pinkie," says Noreen.

"You tell me what you want to say and I'll type it in for you." Pinkie's eyes lock with hers.

"Where's your typewriter?" Dan demands.

"The l'l'library."

"Library? Wher'the fuck's that? I'm not going all the way over there. Shit, let's just forget the whole thing."

"No, no, there's a library here," Pinkie reassures them, "On the other side of the square."

"You're not going to ask me to come in, are you?" Dan says when they reach the building.

"It's just a library," Noreen admonishes.

"You going to need me for anything?" Dan asks.

"I . .I need you for a few questions," Pinkie says diffidently.

"Come in. Just for a little while. Please," Noreen coaxes.

Dan grabs her around the waist, hugs her. "Sure thing, honeybunch."

For once Dan seems restrained, as if in entering the building he has surrendered a little of his boisterous personality. "Let's take a piss first," he says quietly to Pinkie, his whisper revealing the depth of his fear.

Two homeless men already occupy the bathroom—one white and one black. The black man, stripped to the waist, is using a wad of paper towels to dry under each arm. The tile floor around him is covered with water. The white man stands by the urinals waiting his turn at the basin. He smiles amiably at the new arrivals.

"I need to take a piss," Dan announces, shouldering the white man aside from the urinal. "You guys live pretty fancy," Dan calls back over his shoulder.

"We got the bes' of everythin'," the black man replies laughing.

The crisp crease of a pair of hand-tailored suit pants appears briefly in the doorway; the men hear a sniff of disgust and then the pant leg disappears.

"Well, fuck him," the black man says.

"Fuck 'em all," says Dan.

"What you staring at?" Dan says to the slender white man as he turns from the urinal. The man looks up startled; apparently, his thoughts have been far away. A faint smile lingers despite his fear, that of a drunk with the good fortune to latch on to that one timely drink.

Dan hasn't bothered to zip himself up yet, in fact, he is only beginning to tuck himself back into his pants, when he throws an arm around Pinkie's shoulders. "Fucking queers are everywhere," he says to Pinkie, "You ain't queer are you? 'Course not. Noreen wouldn't have nutting to do with no queer.

"You're going to give Noreen a good time, same as me, right." He gives Pinkie's shoulders a squeeze.

Pinkie nods speechless, wanting to break free.

"Only one thing, you got to promise me . . ." Dan moves in front of Pinkie, arm still around Pinkie's shoulders, face only inches away. Pinkie can smell his foul breath, see the several gaps in Dan's mouth where teeth have been yanked or broken free. "You'll wait six months till the divorce is final. Till then I keep doing it, O.K."

Pinkie pushes Dan away from him. He turns and walks out of the tiny bathroom. Surprisingly—Pinkie has had time now to think about what Dan's reaction to the push might be—Dan follows quietly.

"We've got to make copies of these forms," Pinkie says when they reach the room with the typewriters.

"Sure we do," Dan agrees, "We'll do that after we've filled them in. Make a copy for everybody."

Pinkie tries to explain the need for copies, loses track of his explanation, and starts all over again. Dan enjoys his confusion. "You're not going to make mistakes are you?" He glares at Pinkie through hooded eyes.

"Stop giving him a hard time," Noreen interjects. "If he needs copies, we'll make copies." She pauses, "Give him the money," she says, "he needs change."

"Don't look at me," Dan says, "I already paid for the forms."

"Cheap bastard," Noreen says.

"Who you calling a bastard?" Dan grabs Noreen's arm.

"Hey." The deep voice comes from a tall broad-shouldered attorney who is pouring over a set of law books at a nearby table. Dan releases Noreen's arm and glares at the man.

The man looks physically fit, his shoulders broad and fleshed out from evenings in the gym. Certainly, he is bigger than Dan and perhaps equally strong. Dan chokes back what he was about to say and gives the man a second evil look. The man ignores him.

"You want copies, you pay for them yourself," Dan says to Noreen. His words are brave but his voice is pitched two decibels lower than before.

"Sure," Noreen says, "Come on Pinkie."

Pinkie takes a single tentative step. "You have money?" he asks, afraid she will say no.

"Enough to make copies." She smiles, a bright engaging smile, as if his own mother were smiling at him.

"B'but we need Dan," Pinkie says, "I still have to ask him some questions."

"I'll give you the answers Pinkie, best as I can." The smile comes out again. She waits until Pinkie turns toward the copying machine before slowly rubbing her wrist where Dan grabbed her.

They need a second quarter to operate the typewriter. Pinkie takes his time, carefully lining up the forms and the carbons in the typewriter before he announces he is ready for Noreen to put the quarter in. She turns the knob; they hear it click. "Nothing's happening," Pinkie says, "It won't start."

"You've got to turn the handle a second time," interjects a short, elderly woman who is making use of the adjacent typewriter.

"Thanks," Pinkie says.

Noreen smiles at the woman, "you've been a big help."

"Just figured it out myself a minute ago," the woman says. She inhales deeply, then looks around the room, puzzled. Apparently, she does not like what she smells. Another minute goes by and she has found the source of the aroma. She goes back to her typing but the expression on her face says she would rather be someplace else, some place where people like Noreen and Pinkie can't come.

I'm ashamed, Pinkie thinks, so ashamed. . . .

Noreen's divorce entails far more work than Pinkie expected. Dan makes Pinkie chase him across the square twice before he deigns to affix his signature to the forms. Each time Pinkie confronts him, he is subjected to a series of physical and psychological tortures as Dan clowns for the benefit of his equally malevolent male colleagues.

With a pang of fear, Pinkie sees that the silver-haired man with the knife has caught up with them and is standing by Dan's side, ready to act on Dan's slightest impulse.

"I need money for the divorce, Dan," Pinkie says bravely.

"You can't have it."

"I need thirty-five dollars. That's what it costs. You got to give them thirty-five dollars when you file the papers." Pinkie does not know where he got the courage to speak so boldly.

Dan snorts, "You want money, sell your blood." There is a long dramatic pause, then "Or, maybe we'll sell it for you." The crowd of men laughs.

"You don't understand," Pinkie says. He watches from outside his body; he cannot believe he is still there talking to them when every nerve screams he must get away.

"Show him," Dan says.

The silver-haired man pulls back his shirt revealing the knife. Suddenly, without warning the group close in on Pinkie and begin to strike and kick at him. A sharp disabling blow at the back of Pinkie's leg does the most damage. When he stands up again, he is limping.

Pinkie limps back across the plaza, leaving the crowd of men laughing and chattering behind him. They haven't experienced such excitement in a long time; they are pumped up, slapping one another's outstretched palms, elated and grateful for Dan's presence. He acknowledges their accolades.

Pinkie mutters to himself, "He doesn't understand. I've got to get this divorce for Noreen. I don't have the money. She needs the money." His leg hurts where the man kicked him, but he isn't thinking of the pain. He is thinking of Noreen. He almost bumps into her. "I don't have the money," he says.

"I didn't think he would," Noreen says as if talking to herself.

Pinkie twists his fingers together, cracking his knuckles; embarrassed by the sound, he looks down at the concrete.

"Don't worry Pinkie, I have the money." She turns and reaches under her sweater, prying at her bra. When her fingers reemerge, they hold a crumpled stack of bills.

Pinkie says excitedly, "You've got the money. You can get the divorce."

"Yes, Pinkie." But Noreen looks across the plaza, to where Dan and his friends are standing next to the entrance to the courthouse, and wonders if she can.

With Noreen's thirty-five dollars folded in his palm, Pinkie moves slowly across the square toward the entrance. Time itself seems to have slowed, to have become visible and tangible, as anticipation merges with event:

He sees the row on row of dull metal shopping carts filled with the possessions of the homeless, each cart topped with the identical, silver-colored blanket.

He sees Dan and the silver-haired man move slowly to stand in his path, Dan laughing, both men's faces completely free from worry, while Pinkie's own body is bowed down with responsibility, the thirty-five dollars that mean a fresh life for Noreen heavy in his hand.

The orange-haired woman spins into his view a second time, short, no more than 5'3" or 5'4," pretty hair, a full bosom, very attractive, her face and figure serene and competent. "Pinkie," she says.

"Hello, Mrs. Arneson," he replies, remembering her now.

"Miss, or Ms. How have you been Pinkie?"

Dan steps boldly toward them. "We've got to talk to him," he says, jerking his hand toward Pinkie.

Ms Arneson looks Dan up and down as if she has seen similar men before. Though shorter than Dan by four or five inches, she somehow makes it appear it is she who is staring down on him. "I don't think so," she says and returns her attention to Pinkie.

"I'm going to get a divorce," Pinkie says.

"I didn't know you were married."

"Oh, it's n'n'not for me," he stammers, blushing; he knows that Mrs. Arneson knows he goes to singles' dances and he does not want her to think less of him, "it's for her." Noreen steps shyly forward and almost curtsies in the presence of the other woman. The two stare at each other appraisingly.

"Maybe we should walk inside the court house together," Ms. Arneson says to Pinkie, "Then you can tell me all about what you've been doing. You haven't come by for a couple of weeks."

Noreen gives Pinkie a strange look. Because of the red-haired woman's interest, he has grown in stature in Noreen's eyes. She is experiencing a new and unexpected set of emotions.

Dan shakes his fist. "You come back here," he cries, "Both of you." Dan's companions have walked away, disappeared one by one along the edges of the square. For the moment, he is all alone in the center of the plaza shouting.

The Dolphins

The dolphins swim around and among the surfers, amusing some, annoying others.

I swoop out over the lip of a wave, hang ten, do everything the boys do.

Did you see me Victor?

Ignoring me, he shouts, “One of ‘m let me pat’m on the head.”

Every day, fewer boys come with their boards and there are more of the gray shapes. I’m still the only girl.

The dolphin with the crooked fin, White Spot, brushes by me. We mount the next wave together, two riding as one. I bump against him, lose my balance, pearl, am lost in a sea of foam.

When I rise, Victor has disappeared.

www.ingramcontent.com/pod-product-compliance
Lightning Source LLC
LaVergne TN
LVHW051010080826
845145LV00009B/2553

* 9 7 8 0 9 8 4 1 6 0 3 9 6 *